# MOVING TO HOPE

PJ FIALA

# COPYRIGHT

Copyright © 2014 by PJ Fiala

All rights reserved. This book or any portion thereof may not be reproduced or used in any manner whatsoever without the express written permission of the publisher except for the use of brief quotations in a book review.

**Publisher's note:** This is a work of fiction. Names, characters, places, and incidents either are the product of the author's imagination or are used fictitiously. Any resemblance to actual events, locales, or persons, living or dead, is entirely coincidental.

Printed in the United States of America

First published 2015

Rolling Thunder Publishing

Fiala, PJ

Moving to Hope / PJ Fiala

p. cm.

1. Romance—Fiction. 2. Contemporary—Fiction. I. Title

**Paperback**

**ISBN-13:** 978-1-942618-13-3

# DEDICATION

I dedicate this book to all of our men and women who have served in the military, police, firefighters, EMTs and any profession which requires sacrifice of life and limb. These are true heroes and they often go unnoticed.
Thank you.

# LET'S STAY IN TOUCH

Let's stay in touch where bots, algorithms and subjective admins don't decide what we see. PJ Fiala's Readers' Club is my newsletter where I promise to only send you content you enjoy! https://www.subscribepage.com/pjfialafm

# 1

## THE WEDDING

Emily sobbed and raised her hand to her mouth. Tears formed in her eyes. "You look so beautiful, Joci. That dress is perfect, just perfect."

Joci smiled. "Thank you. It feels perfect." And it did. She'd waited a long time to get married. Forty-five years to be exact.

The other girls chatted and talked excitedly. There was a knock on the door and a beautiful dark-haired, blue-eyed woman walked into the room.

"Hi, can I come in and take pictures?"

"Yes, Molly, come in and meet everyone," Joci said, walking forward to greet her.

"Molly, this is Emily, Jeremiah's mom. Staci, Angie, and Erin are Jeremiah's sisters-in-law. You know my sister, Jackie, and my best friend, Sandi. Everyone, this is Molly Bates. I met Molly a few years back at a class and then again on the Veteran's Ride, where she was one of the photographers. We've been working on a few things together since then. She freelances and I was thrilled that she was available today."

"Hello everyone, it's great to meet you. Okay, let's start getting some pictures, shall we? Then, while you're putting the finishing touches on, I'll go out and take pictures of the guys."

She loved taking pictures, especially at weddings. Everyone was so happy and beautiful in their formal clothing. Most people were polite and used their best manners at weddings. Even the biggest bridezillas settled down by the time the wedding actually arrived.

"Joci, you're a beautiful bride. You look radiant." Molly smiled. She snapped pictures of the veil being pinned on Joci's head, Jeremiah's mom buttoning the cuffs on her bridal gown, and Sandi placing a necklace around Joci's neck—the usual photographs brides wanted to be frozen in time for the days when the memories begin to fade.

Joci beamed. "Thank you, Molly. I have a hard time believing this is actually happening. I'm forty-five and a first-time bride. I'd given up on love before I met Jeremiah."

"Well, I'm so glad you found each other." She smiled as she motioned for the women to stand behind a bouquet of flowers. "I love taking pictures of happy people. And these pictures...well, they're going to be amazing; you're a gorgeous family."

She positioned the women in various poses and snapped dozens of pictures as she enjoyed the excited chatter; the fragrance of fresh flowers, the ladies' perfumes, and wedding day happiness filled the air. "Okay, I'm heading down the hall to snap some pictures of the men. I'll see you at the altar, Joci." She gave a small wave and slipped out the door.

Locating room number three, she knocked on the door and poked in her head. Jeremiah saw her and waved her in. He met her halfway across the room and hugged her briefly. "Thank you for taking pictures for us today. Joci and I are thrilled you were available."

She smiled. "I'm excited beyond belief to be here. I love Joci." She glanced around the room, looking for the perfect spot for photos. The lighting was good, the room was decorated similarly to the room Joci and her family were in with tan armchairs, tan carpeting, and oil paintings of flowers hung on each wall.

Jeremiah smiled and turned to introduce her to the rest of the guys. "Everyone, I would like you to meet our photographer, Molly Bates. These handsome men are my brothers, Dayton, Tommy, and Bryce, and this is our father, Thomas."

Walking to the four men standing by a tall table, he said, "These are my buddies: Sarge, Superman, Pitbull, and Radio."

Jeremiah turned them to the corner of the room where the groomsmen helped each other with cuff links and cravats. Continuing with the introductions, he said, "David is Joci's brother-in-law. And these are my sons: JT, Gunnar, and Ryder."

Molly looked at the camera in her hands as her cheeks brightened pink. "Okay. Ummm, let's start over here." She pointed to an area in the corner. With shaking hands, she set up her tripod across the room. She placed the men in several positions and snapped numerous pictures.

"Okay, Ryder and JT, if you could sit on the stools; and Gunnar, if you would stand between, but just behind them, please," she said, a catch in her throat. She looked through her lashes as the men took up their positions. Mostly, she watched Ryder. She leaned in to look through the lens of her camera and felt goose bumps run up and down her spine as Ryder's intense green eyes trained on her. She repositioned the guys a couple more times and snapped several more pictures.

"Okay Jeremiah, why don't you step in next to Gunnar for a few pictures?"

She found it difficult to continue working as her mind kept wandering to Ryder. Each time she looked at him, he was staring right at her.

"Dayton and Sarge, let's get you two with Jeremiah, please."

Molly briefly glanced at Ryder and watched him slowly run his hand across his jaw and back to the nape of his neck. His eyes caught Molly's almost immediately, causing her heart to pound in her chest. Quickly grabbing her camera tripod with her left hand, she snapped a few more pictures.

"It's time to go, Jeremiah," Dayton announced.

Relief washing over her, Molly gathered up her cameras and equipment. "Thanks, guys; I'll see you out there," she called as she quickly headed out the door, her pulse racing and her temperature higher than it had been before walking into that room. It had little to do with the fact that she was in a room filled with handsome men, but more because one of those men had caught her attention in a serious way.

R yder watched Molly walk out the door and had the desire to follow her. Her eyes were stunning—so shiny and blue—like a bright summer sky. Her dark hair was cut in a short bob. It suited her. He wondered if it was soft. He wanted to touch it and let it fall through his fingers. She was petite but taller than his mom, even in the flat-heeled shoes she wore today, but he thought her legs would look incredible in high heels, wrapped around his waist as he pushed himself into her. He took a deep breath then released it, shaking his head; he didn't even know if she was single, so no need to continue torturing himself.

"Hey Ryder, you ready to go?" JT chuckled.

"Yeah, I'm coming," he mumbled. He swiped his hand across his jaw and looked away from his brother.

JT nudged him with his arm. "She's fucking hot. You gonna tap that?"

Ryder scowled at him. "Don't be crude, JT."

Gunnar shrugged his shoulders and smirked. "Well, your eyes never left her once. You looked at her like you were going to devour her. Poor thing looked nervous."

Laughing, JT said, "Maybe I'll take a shot at her if Ryder's too shy to talk to her."

Ryder glared at JT just as Jeremiah approached.

"Come on boys; I'm getting married." Jeremiah wrapped his arm around Ryder's neck and pulled him forward toward the door. "You okay?"

"Yeah. I'm okay, Dad."

"Don't let them get you down, buddy."

Ryder nodded.

He and JT sat in the church with their grandparents. Gunnar was walking his mom down the aisle, so he headed down the hall toward the chapel doors to meet up with his mom, Aunt Jackie, and his mom's best friend, Sandi.

As Ryder and JT took their seats, he looked around to find Molly. His heart hammered in his chest when he found her standing in the corner at the front of the church, waiting for the men to walk out so she could take pictures. Her dark hair shined where the lights touched it. Her slender body stood tall as she set her camera on top of the tripod and adjusted the lens. She glanced his way, and his heart sped up; heat crawled up his torso and beaded on his forehead.

M olly's heart beat wildly. There was something about Ryder that got to her. She chanced a look around and saw Ryder staring at her and her breath caught in her throat as little shivers danced down her arms and up her spine. Dammit, she couldn't stop looking at him. She forced herself to look away just as the men walked through the door to stand in front of the church. She almost missed it! She had to start concentrating.

She snapped pictures of the men as the music started, then quickly trotted around the back of the pews and scrambled through to catch the bridesmaids walking up the aisle. She could snap posed pictures later, but sometimes these in-the-moment shots were fantastic. Joci and Gunnar began walking in. Gunnar looked at her and winked, and she clicked away. As soon as they walked past her, she scrambled around to run up the side of the church to get more candid moments up front. As she reached the front of the church, she was able to capture Gunnar and Jeremiah hugging and then she looked over and saw Ryder hugging Joci. Her fingers were tapping the camera buttons as quickly as she could while she watched Ryder whisper something in Joci's ear. JT leaned in next and hugged Joci as Ryder hugged his dad. Wow, what a moment.

Throughout the ceremony, she continued taking pictures of this beautiful family. She couldn't wait to get home and take a closer look at Ryder. One of the advantages of being a photographer was knowing you could snap away now and stare all you wanted to later —in private.

Joci had given Molly a list of pictures she wanted to have taken after the ceremony. After the honeymoon, she and Joci would sit down and work on the photo albums together. Joci wanted a few pictures for the house, but mostly, she wanted digital collections made. She and Jeremiah planned to give digital picture frames to all of their family and friends to share memories from today and throughout the past year.

She ticked through the picture list she'd gotten from Joci. Having just finished with Sandi and Jon and their kids, she leaned over the pew to see who was next in line on her list. She could feel the air around her crackle and goose bumps shimmied up her arms. She slowly raised her eyes and looked into Ryder's. She sucked in a breath and froze. Gawd, he was beautiful. Having him this close to her was very distracting. She could smell the spicy, tantalizing scent of his after-shave and see his corded neck and strong jaw leading to his broad shoulders. Wow!

"I believe my brothers and I are next," he said, his voice husky and low.

Molly's mouth went dry, and she had difficulty swallowing. When Joci had described the boys to her, she had explained that Ryder was shy and would need encouragement to participate in things. He didn't usually jump in unless invited—he was content to stand back and wait to be asked. So Molly was a bit surprised that he approached her at all. When the only response she gave was a slight nod, Ryder's eyebrows shot up in question.

Licking her lips, Molly replied, "Yes, you're up next."

R yder continued watching her. She had the most beautiful eyes he had ever seen—set off perfectly by her dark brown hair. Standing this close to her, he could smell her perfume. She smelled like...more. His cock twitched as he watched her swipe her little pink tongue across her lips. Now that she was ready to take pictures of him and his brothers, his cock decided to stand at attention.

"Maybe we can start on the altar and then we'll step outside for a few more pictures your parents asked for." Her voice shook, and a blush crept up her cheeks.

His brothers chuckled behind him as Ryder nodded at Molly and headed toward the altar. He turned to scowl at them. He loved them, but they could be dickheads when they wanted to be. When he reached the altar and turned to face the back of the church, he found Molly standing right in front of him. Good thing he was wearing a tuxedo to help camouflage the growing tent in his pants. He grimaced at his brothers as they stood watching him, then turned his attention back to Molly.

~

"Okay, Gunnar, if you would sit on the stool, and JT and Ryder, you two stand just behind him. We'll do a few formal pictures, then some fun ones." The boys moved into position as Molly looked through her lens. She snapped a few pictures, moved them around again and continued until she had the shots she wanted.

These guys were great subjects. She could easily do something like this for Rolling Thunder. She made a mental note to mention this to Joci. She hadn't had a chance to photograph these guys at the Veteran's Ride, because the studio that hired her had assigned her to one of the Veterans groups that had recently earned accolades for their work with veterans. That group had also been a recipient of some of the money from the ride.

After finishing with the boys alone, Jeremiah and Joci came forward to be included in some of the pictures with them.

Molly arranged them in several poses and clicked away. Ryder watched her intently. It was unnerving the way he continued to focus on her, and she wondered when her hands would stop shaking. After finishing with the pictures indoors, they headed outside for some special shots. Molly grabbed her camera and started to reach for her big camera bag when Ryder stepped in and grabbed it for her. Without saying a word, he walked toward the back of the church with her bag. She watched him a few beats and looked back to see Joci smiling at her. Her cheeks flamed bright red as she turned and walked in the direction Ryder had gone.

Joci looked up at Jeremiah. "I do believe I see some sparks flying."

"Yep. We'll see what happens from here. They sure seem to be paying a lot of attention to each other," Jeremiah smirked.

They both chuckled and followed Ryder and Molly out the door.

Joci had not only fallen in love with Jeremiah at the Veteran's Ride this summer but also with an old orange 1937 Ford Pickup with an oak box and oak box rails. Jeremiah had asked the old guy who owned it if he could rent it for the wedding. He told Jeremiah he would be happy to rent it to him, but he would prefer it if Jeremiah bought it and took it off his hands; he'd been thinking about selling it anyway. Jeremiah was excited when he found out the old truck was for sale. Joci was about to find out that Jeremiah not only bought the old truck, but he'd bought it for her. Molly couldn't wait to capture Joci's surprise in pictures.

"Okay, line up alongside the truck for a few group pictures," Molly directed. Everyone else in attendance knew what was coming. Jeremiah lifted Joci into the box of the truck for a few photos. The boys all took 'gangster' style pictures with the truck and joked around.

"I'd like some pictures with Joci sitting in the driver's seat," Jeremiah said. He kneeled down in front of her for a few photos, then he reached into his pocket and pulled out the truck keys, with a tag attached, and wrapped in a ribbon. He held them up to her with a smile stretched across his face. Joci looked at the keys, carefully taking them in her hand, and reading the tag—"*Something old. I love you, Joci – Jeremiah.*"

Joci gasped and threw her hand up to her mouth. Molly snapped picture after picture as Joci's face ran through a gamut of emotions expressing her surprise and happiness.

Joci sprang from the truck and jumped into Jeremiah's arms as he swung her around and whispered in her ear, "I love you, Jocelyn Sheppard, with everything I have in me."

"God. I love you, Jeremiah, so much. Thank you. Is it mine? Is that what this means?"

"Yes, baby, it's your wedding present."

"Oh my God, Jeremiah, it...it's perfect."

All who stood by watching clapped, cheered, and wiped tears from their eyes as they watched. Except for Ryder; he watched Molly.

Once all the pictures had been taken, the wedding party and guests headed to the reception hall. Molly began loading her gear into her car, taking deep breaths to get her emotions under control. She was captivated by Ryder in a big way, but she had no business getting lost in a man, even this gorgeous man. No way! *Focus, Molly, just focus.*

At the reception, she took pictures of the wedding party eating dinner, dancing, the bride and groom's first dance, cutting the cake, throwing the bouquet, and throwing the garter. Now she was done. She loved her job, but after taking thousands of pictures today, she was wiped out. The day had been both emotional and energizing. She packed up her gear and slipped out the back door to go home.

The drive home was a blur. She thought about Ryder. He was possibly the most handsome man she had ever met. Her heart beat faster just thinking about him now. She wanted to get home, pour a glass of wine, and look at her pictures.

She walked into her kitchen and set her camera bags on the counter. She pulled disks out of her bag and fired up her tablet. She could download the pictures onto her tablet while she jumped into the shower, then she would sit and enjoy looking at Ryder.

After her shower and her glass of wine had been poured, she grabbed her tablet and sat on the sofa. She began browsing through the pictures from today. Joci was easy to please, but these were going to make her ecstatic. All she wanted was to camouflage her injuries. She had been in a bad motorcycle accident about five weeks ago. They had just learned that Joci was pregnant, so it had been a very stressful time for their family. She didn't lose the baby and was recovering, but her right arm, shoulder, and her collar bone were severely damaged. Her right hip wasn't broken, but badly and deeply bruised. Her slight limp was noticeable when she was tired. She still couldn't lift her right arm up, and was supposed to be wearing a soft cast, but refused to for the wedding. Joci had asked Molly to make sure she didn't look injured in the pictures. She didn't want to look back on this day and remember the accident—just the day she became Jeremiah's wife.

Molly stopped on the first photo of Ryder. Her breath caught in her throat. Jesus, he wasn't just beautiful; he was perfect. His shoulders appeared larger than they probably were in his tuxedo but still broad. He was tall, nicely built, and freaking handsome. Wow! He had a slight smirk on his face, and those blazing green eyes were staring right at her. She looked at his picture for a long time, finally making herself swipe her finger across the screen, moving to the next one. There he was again. And again and again and again. She had taken tons of pictures of him. No wonder JT and Gunnar had been smirking at her all day.

She fell asleep on the sofa holding her tablet, looking at Ryder's picture. Would anyone ever capture her attention like he had?

R yder kept his eyes on Molly all night. He wanted to ask her out, wanted to ask her to stay. He just couldn't. She seemed interested in him; every time he looked at her today, she was staring right back at him. Watching the pulsing in her neck unnerved him, imagining he was doing that to her. It was maddening, wanting to approach her and not being able to. At the church, he could talk about the pictures or the wedding. Now, though, wanting to ask her out, he just couldn't bring himself to do it. Women always approached Ryder; he never had to approach them. He didn't know what to do now; it sure didn't help that JT and Gunnar were making fun of him at every turn. Jerks.

He looked over to see Molly slip out the back door with her gear. He waited, hoping she would come back in and have a drink, but she never came back. Fuck! The remainder of the night, Ryder visited with his family. He had always enjoyed spending time with his cousins, so he walked over to a table where a bunch of them were sitting and joined them. His mind was elsewhere, though—on a beautiful, dark-haired woman with bright blue eyes.

# 2

## THE MORNING AFTER

Ryder woke up with a headache. After Molly had left the wedding last night, he began drinking away his irritation. He was irritated with himself for not having the courage to ask her out. He hated being shy. He always had. There wasn't much he could do about it, though; it was just him. Neither of his brothers were shy, none of his uncles were shy, and his biological mother sure as hell wasn't shy. Why the heck did *he* have to be shy? He could peptalk himself all damn day long, but as soon as it came time to ask a girl out, he froze. He had mentioned this to Joci one day when she was home recovering from her accident.

"When the right girl comes along, Ryder, you'll be willing to move heaven and earth to get to know her. You'll see. In the meantime, maybe write things down in a notebook."

"What things?"

"Well...how you feel. A conversation you would like to have with someone. It might make you feel like you've already had that conversation and the person won't feel like a stranger. I do that when I'm frustrated. I'll write a letter and then tuck it away. I never send it, but I feel like I've gotten something off my chest."

"I hate writing. Maybe...I'll think about it."

Well, if last night was any indication, his mom was wrong. He didn't have the courage to ask Molly out, and he'd never reacted to a woman like he had to her. He was twenty-six-years-old, and he didn't want to wait until he was forty-five to find his soul mate like his dad had. After listening to Jeremiah go on and on about Joci these past few months, Ryder wanted that now. He hated being alone. He hated going out with his brothers and watching them leave with women. The only time he left the bar with a woman was when she was bold enough to approach him. He had been approached enough in his time, but it was just sex, and the next day he moved on. He had nothing to talk about with these women, and there was nothing about them he cared to know.

Molly, he wanted to know. He wanted to know what she liked and what she did on a day-to-day basis. He wanted to watch her eat and laugh and sleep, and he wanted to watch her face while he fucked her. That's what he wanted. When he saw her packing up last night, he just couldn't make himself go and talk to her. So fucking frustrating.

～

**M**olly woke up with a stiff neck. She'd slept on the sofa all night, holding on to her tablet with a picture of Ryder staring at her. Was she a fool? He hadn't asked her out, even though she thought he was interested. He was probably used to women throwing themselves at him. Well, she wasn't going to throw herself at anyone. She was going to do her job and move on. She would spend today working on the pictures and culling out the bad ones. Then she'd call Joci and let her know the pictures were ready for her, and they could make arrangements for getting the pictures to her. After that, Molly would move on from Ryder Sheppard.

She got up and made herself a cup of coffee and began looking through the pictures with a photographer's eye, not through the eyes of a silly girl with her first crush. She wasn't going to make the same mistakes her mom had.

～

"Hey there, you look sad. What's up?" Joci asked Ryder as she sat on the sofa next to him.

"Nothing. Everything. I don't know, Mom. Fuck, I'm frustrated." Ryder's jaw clenched as he sat forward, elbows on his knees.

They had finished opening gifts at Emily and Thomas's house. Ryder snuck off to the living room because he didn't feel the best and he definitely didn't feel like talking to anyone. Joci was tired and had slipped away to the living room to rest for a little while and found Ryder sitting there by himself.

"Aww, now you have to tell me what's up. You can't leave me hanging."

He let out a long breath and sat back.

"Remember when you and I talked about me being shy, and you said when the right woman came along I would move heaven and earth to get to know her?"

Joci smiled. "Of course, I remember."

"You were wrong. Last night I couldn't bring myself to ask Molly out. I watched her pack up, and I wanted to go over and ask her out so bad, but I just couldn't do it."

Joci reached over and patted his knee. "Yes, we saw the sparks flying. Timing is everything, you know. Don't put so much pressure on yourself. Maybe last night wasn't the right time. Did you write it down?"

"No. I got drunk instead." He smirked.

"How'd that work for you?" She smirked right back.

He scraped his hands through his short spiky hair. "Dammit, I hate being me sometimes."

They sat quietly for some time; he didn't bother to respond. Joci leaned back and closed her eyes. Ryder did the same. His head still hurt a little, and he didn't know what to do with himself. Sitting here quietly with his mom felt good.

"There you two are. What's up?"

"Boy, everyone's sure being nosy today," Ryder snapped.

"Excuse me?" Jeremiah snapped back. "All I asked is what's up. Everyone else is outside or eating in the kitchen."

"Geez, never mind." Ryder stood up and walked out of the room.

Joci looked at Jeremiah and smirked. "He's mad at himself for not asking Molly out last night. And I think he's a little hung over."

Jeremiah nodded. He sat down next to Joci on the sofa. "Well, who knew he would be so moody?"

Joci laughed. "If you're correct, and this little bump I have is a girl, you'll get all kinds of moody in about thirteen years or so."

"Oh my God, what have we done?" Jeremiah grinned. "If you're by my side, I can handle anything." Joci laid her head on Jeremiah's shoulder and closed her eyes. "I love you, Jeremiah."

"I love you, too, babe."

Joci's phone rang and Jeremiah helped her reach into her back pocket to grab it. Having put her soft cast back on, she was still a little clumsy trying to do that herself.

"Hello...Hi, Molly. How are you?" Joci looked at Jeremiah and grinned.

"Absolutely, when do you want to get together? Yes, we'll be back next Saturday. Why don't I call you a week from tomorrow and we'll take a look? I'm excited to see them. Thank you for being there yesterday. Yes, we'll have a great time. Talk to you next week. Bye, Molly."

She turned to Jeremiah. "Well, if Ryder can't come up with the courage to ask Molly out while we're gone, maybe we can work something out when we get back. If it's meant to be, it'll happen."

# 3

## HE DIDN'T CALL

"You know moping around isn't going to help, right?" Gunnar asked.

"Fuck, Gunnar, don't start busting my chops, okay?" Ryder responded in a huff.

"Man, I'm not busting your chops. You've been moping around for five damn days now. I'm just saying, don't get down, get busy. Give her a call. Maybe it'll be easier over the phone. What's the worst that can happen? She can say no? Big fucking deal, there are other women out there."

"Easy for you to say. Molly's different. I've never had these feelings for a woman before. I'm afraid I'll screw it up."

"Well, sitting here isn't going to change it. Call her up, ask her to dinner. Take her somewhere you can talk, but also where something else is going on in case you run out of things to say."

"Yeah, and where is that?"

"How about that restaurant in Green Bay where they cook your food on a hibachi? There's a little dinner show while the chef is preparing your meal and you can talk while you eat. If you can't think of anything to say, you can talk about the cook or the food. Just sayin'."

Gunnar got up to walk to the kitchen as he tapped out a text. It was Friday morning, and they had to get to work. He poured himself and Ryder a cup of coffee and took Ryder's cup out to sit on the coffee table in front of him. He laid a piece of paper down next to the coffee cup.

"I'm taking off for work. I've got a lot to do today. I promised Nelson I would have his bike finished so he could get another ride in this year. Mom and Dad will be home tomorrow, and I want to get their lawn mowed before they do so Dad doesn't have to do it. I'm leaving work early today to head over there. See you later, man."

"Okay. See ya."

Ryder looked at the piece of paper Gunnar set down next to his coffee cup. A number was written down on it and a name...*Molly*. How the hell did Gunnar get Molly's phone number? Ryder ran his hands through his hair, grabbed his cup of coffee, and sat back into the sofa. Gunnar had a good point; he should call her. That way if she turned him down, it wouldn't be so embarrassing. In the meantime, he was going to try writing this all down as his mom suggested.

**M**olly paced back and forth in her living room. Tammy, Molly's best friend since kindergarten, was sitting on Molly's sofa with a cup of coffee in her hand and Molly's tablet on her lap. Ryder's picture was staring right back at her.

"He's scorching, Molly. Wow, look at his eyes. I can see why you can't get him out of your head; talk about hot dreams!"

"You're supposed to be telling me he isn't worth it and to not be like my mom—not encouraging me to want him."

Tammy grinned. She knew Molly better than Molly knew herself sometimes.

"I don't think you need any encouragement in wanting him. And for the record, you aren't like your mom. You need to stop comparing yourself to her. You're amazing, Molly. You're beautiful, smart, and creative. You're making it on your own. Stop damning yourself to a lonely life because you don't want to be like your mom."

"I know, Tammy; I do. But I've struggled for so long. I grew up watching my mom struggle. Besides, as soon as he finds out what I really am, he isn't going to want to be with me anyway."

Molly grabbed her tablet and looked at Ryder's beautiful face and body. His eyes were so mesmerizing. The green was so green, and his lashes were long and a little darker than his hair, creating a beautiful frame. His lips were full and looked soft, probably would feel fabulous kissing her. He had a strong jaw and a great smile—what a package. Just looking at him caused her heart to beat faster. She was close enough to him when taking their pictures that she caught a few whiffs of his cologne. She could still smell him and imagined what it would feel like to be wrapped in his arms. Without thinking, Molly began tracing his picture with her finger.

"What happened to you is in your past. It was also not in your control. You have to stop blaming yourself and thinking everyone on earth will judge you for it." Tammy sucked in a deep breath. "Maybe you should give him a call. You said he was shy—maybe he's too shy to ask you out."

"Joci told me he was shy, but he didn't seem shy at the wedding. As a matter of fact, he approached me at one point to ask me if it was time for his pictures. And then, he carried my bag outside when we walked out to take pictures. I saw him dancing with some woman, too. So, I don't know what to think about the shy part."

"Well, first of all, he wouldn't be shy around his family. So, you weren't observing him in a situation where you could judge that fairly. Second of all, he asked you about taking his picture, which was something he knew the answer to already. And, you said he carried your bag out, but didn't say anything to you, just picked it up and started walking. I would say shy."

"Well, I'm not going to call him. If he really wanted to get to know me, he would man up and call me. Besides, it's probably for the best anyway."

"Molly, I will kick your ass if you don't stop condemning yourself. You need to listen to me. What can I do to get that through your head? Of the two of us, I'm the one who has made stupid mistakes, not you," Tammy said. "Let's go out next weekend and have some fun. Maybe you'll meet someone else, and you'll stop thinking about Ryder Sheppard."

Taking a deep breath and letting it out slowly, Molly absently answered her, "Yeah. Sure."

# 4

## STILL SHY

Ryder sat with his phone in his hand. He had nine digits dialed in and then he hesitated. He sucked in a deep breath and slowly let it out. As he exhaled, he hit the button and canceled the call. Nope, it didn't feel right. He would think about it today and call her later. He got up, slipped the piece of paper with Molly's number into his pocket, and headed out to get on his bike. The fresh air would clear his head and help him think. Nothing like a bike ride to help a person sort through their thoughts.

Pulling into the parking lot at Rolling Thunder, he drove to the rear garage door closest to his workstation. He parked his bike next to Gunnar's and went in through the back door. They each had their own stations with their tools and lifts. Ryder, Gunnar, and Frog were the primary mechanics. They had a couple of students from the local tech school who worked part-time doing oil and spark plug changes. Their workstations were pushed to the back of the shop. As the company was growing, the building was bursting at the seams. His dad had been talking about adding another addition onto the current building. Dad wanted Joci to have an office here to meet with her clients. She currently used a spare bedroom at the house, but with the baby coming, they were going to need the space. There was a small, unused room upstairs next to Jeremiah's office that could be used in the interim, and once they added on to the building, there would be more room for everyone.

Ryder checked out the bike he'd be working on today and pulled the needed tools out of his toolbox and set them on the lift. Gunnar walked in from the front showroom and nodded at him. Ryder stiffened, thinking he was going to start asking questions about calling Molly.

Instead, he walked over and said, "Tomorrow night is Frog's birthday party at The Barn. You still going?"

Shit! Ryder had forgotten about Frog's birthday. But Frog was a friend, and he wouldn't miss his birthday party.

"Yeah, I'll be there."

He thought about calling Molly and asking her out for tonight instead of tomorrow night, but that seemed wrong. Weren't you supposed to give a girl a little time to prepare? Well, at any rate, he wasn't going to call her today.

～

"A re you riding with us tonight, Ryder?" JT asked.

The three brothers sat around the kitchen table having morning coffee. They all lived together in the house they rented from Joci. When she moved in with Jeremiah, she asked Gunnar if he was interested in renting it. He and JT were talking about moving in together anyway. Ryder had a nice little apartment he liked, so he initially said he wasn't interested. But, after a few weeks, he realized he loved being here with them, so he moved in as well. They each had their own bedroom and plenty of garage space for their vehicles and bikes. It was a great ranch-style house with a full basement that had become their 'party' room. That way they kept the mess downstairs when they had friends over. They had set up a workout room down there, too, which came in handy.

"Nah, I'll take my truck. That way when you guys hook up, I can just slip out."

"Well, you might hook up, too."

Ryder shrugged. "Maybe."

Gunnar walked into the kitchen and poured himself a cup of coffee.

"Mom just called. They're at the airport and will be home in about an hour. Did you guys want to run over and see them this afternoon?"

"Yeah," JT and Ryder said in unison.

"**G**lad you guys are home. Did you have a great time, or aren't we supposed to ask that?" JT asked, smirking at Jeremiah and Joci.

Jeremiah pulled Joci into his side and kissed the top of her head. He looked at the boys and smiled. "We had a great time. We laid on the beach every single day. We didn't really do anything but rest, relax, and talk. We shopped a little bit and saw a couple of dinner shows."

"What's going on around here? Did we miss anything?" Joci asked.

The boys shrugged. "Not much. We didn't burn anything down. The shop is still standing, and everyone that was working at the shop is still working there, so I guess you didn't miss much," Gunnar teased.

Jeremiah leaned down close to Joci's ear, "Told you."

She smiled. "Okay, well, we're having a working lunch on Wednesday this week to finalize the plans for Danny Schaefer's build next weekend. We need you guys there. Pizza for everyone," Joci said.

Danny Schaeffer is the veteran receiving the majority of the proceeds from the Veteran's Ride this year. The purpose of the Veteran's Ride is to help local vets with whatever needs they have. Danny's leg was blown off while in Afghanistan. His two-story house is laid out so the bedroom and bathroom are upstairs. Now they can add a first-floor bedroom and bathroom to his home.

"I'm going to ask Molly to take pictures of the build at Danny's house. We'll need them for the website, and I want to add them to a DVD before I have them burned. That way we can show the ride and then how the proceeds for the ride were used. I also want to get an interview or at least some comments from Danny for the end of the DVD. What do you guys think of that?"

Ryder froze at the sound of Molly's name. She was going to be around next weekend? He would be seeing her again. His heart started beating a rapid tempo in his chest. He'd find a way to ask her out for sure. Yes, this was perfect; he would see her next weekend and find the courage to ask her out.

Joci looked at Ryder. His face took on a look she'd never seen before.

"Ryder? Is that okay with you?" Joci asked.

"Ah, yeah, it's good," Ryder said as his face burned red.

Joci looked at Gunnar with her brows furrowed. Gunnar frowned and shook his head no.

# 5

## THE BARN

"So, what's up with Ryder and Molly?" Joci asked Gunnar.

"So far, nothing. He hasn't called her, even though I gave him her number. Thanks for texting me back so fast. He's frustrated with himself and moped around the house all week. It's good that Molly will be at the build; it'll give Ryder another shot to ask her out."

Joci nodded. "You're welcome. So he still hasn't been able to talk to Molly—poor kid."

"Yeah, I get that he's shy, and it's hard for him, but seriously, he needs to just go for it."

"Well, that's easy for you to say; you aren't shy." Joci walked over to the desk and sat down at her computer. Gunnar shrugged and left the office to get back to work.

∼

J T, Ryder, Gunnar, Joci, Jeremiah, Frog, one of the mechanics at Rolling Thunder, and some of the other employees were standing around a tall table at The Barn celebrating Frog's birthday. By nine-thirty, Joci was stifling a yawn when a tall, leggy blonde walked over and pushed herself between JT and Ryder. She reached over and ran her hand over the spikes on Ryder's hair and whispered something in his ear. Joci raised an eyebrow as she watched Ryder's face turn bright red. He looked down at the table, and the blonde leaned in and whispered something more. Of course, blondie's breasts rubbed against Ryder's arm. Ryder looked up and then stood up completely stiff as his eyes grew large and the color drained from his face.

"Hi Joci, Jeremiah. How're you doing?" Molly glared at the blonde and then shot Ryder a look that could kill.

"Molly, it's so good to see you. How are you? I can't wait to see the pictures." Joci smiled and tried getting Molly's attention.

Molly looked away from Ryder and turned to Joci. "They turned out great; I can't wait for you to see them." Molly motioned to her friends.

"I'd like you to meet my girlfriends. Girls, this is Joci and Jeremiah Sheppard. And, of course, their sons."

To Tammy, Molly said, "Not sure who the woman is with her tongue in Ryder's ear."

Joci heard her and looked at Molly. "She's not with us. She just walked up and started whispering in his ear."

Molly shrugged her shoulders. "Doesn't matter. We're going to go over to the other side and find a table by the dance floor. Can we get together on Monday to look at the pictures? They're amazing, if I do say so myself."

Tammy piped up. "I saw them, and they're perfect. Wow. All I could say was wow!"

Joci smiled. "Thank you. I can't wait. Can you come to Rolling Thunder around ten on Monday?"

Molly didn't hear her. She knew she didn't have any right to be jealous. Ryder didn't call her because she wasn't pretty enough or he wasn't interested. Apparently, he liked them blonde and tall. So, fine. It hurt, though. She had thought about him all week. She had dreamt about him. She woke up two mornings with the sweats; the dreams had been so real. She never thought she was a real beauty. She had boyfriends, but she didn't look like blondie here. Ryder and every other man liked women like this: tall, thin, long blonde hair, and large breasts. Molly needed to get away from the table. She felt sucker-punched; it was hard to breathe, and she felt tears threatening.

"Molly?"

"I'm sorry, Joci. I didn't hear you."

Joci nodded. "How about Monday at ten? At Rolling Thunder?"

She nodded. Tammy pulled on her arm. "Come on girl, let's go shake what God gave you. Nice to meet you all."

With a wave, they were off to the other side of the bar crowding around a table by the dance floor. Tammy quickly pulled Molly out onto the dance floor, and they started shaking their booties.

"Don't let it bother you, Moll. He didn't look interested in her at all; he was staring at you."

"Let's just dance and not think. Maybe tonight I'll get wasted and forget."

"That's my girl."

∾

R yder looked at Joci and shook his head. Women! Blondie leaned in and whispered, "Come on baby, let's get out of here."

"Get lost, Rachel. Not interested."

"Fuck you, Ryder. You weren't saying that two weeks ago. Jerk off!"

Blondie stalked off to her friends. Jeremiah chuckled, and Joci shot him a look.

Ryder looked over at the dance floor where Molly and her friends were dancing. She looked fabulous. She was wearing a short white dress with black polka dots on it and black heels that shouted, 'fuck me.' He could tell she was mad, but he didn't ask Rachel to come over and whisper in his ear. He didn't even know she was here. He hadn't thought of any women since he'd met Molly. Look at her—she was shaking her sweet little ass on the dance floor and smiling with her friends. God, he wanted her to shake that ass against him. His cock swelled just thinking about it.

As the night wore on, Ryder couldn't do anything but watch Molly. A couple of guys had joined her and her friends on the dance floor, and Ryder wanted to go over and push them away. One guy wrapped his arms around her waist and let her wiggle her gorgeous ass against him. That almost killed him. He didn't have any right to be jealous, but damn it, he wanted her. In a weird way, he already thought of her as his.

M olly and her girls were having a great time. She tried in vain not to look over at Ryder. When she couldn't take it anymore, she would spin around on the floor, so it didn't look like she was looking at him. He was always watching her; it made her stomach tighten and her heart leap. He was wearing tight jeans that accented his hard thighs and a tight t-shirt. He had a tattoo going down his right arm that looked like a snake or something. It slid down and around his arm to the elbow, but most of it was tucked under his t-shirt. She wanted to see it—all of it. But he wasn't interested in her, so she would be left wondering about that tattoo. She spun around one more time and there he was with that blonde again, and she had her hand in his front pocket. *Asshole.*

Tammy pulled Molly off the dance floor back to the table where the girls had shots lined up and waiting.

"Drink up, girls. Here's to Saturday night!" Tammy yelled.

They downed their shots. Molly's head started to spin since she'd had a few shots already. She wasn't driving, but still—she didn't want tomorrow to be a total waste. But it was the only way to keep from thinking about that frigging blonde whispering sweet nothings in Ryder's ear. Bitch!

Cara and Suzie pulled Molly out onto the floor for another dance just as a hot guy came to the table and started chatting Tammy up. Molly stumbled a little, and she and her friends started to giggle. A cute sandy-haired man came up behind Molly and slid his arms around her waist as he pulled her back to him.

He leaned down and whispered in her ear, "Let's take off, beautiful. I can think of a few things we could be doing right now that we can't do here on the dance floor."

She stiffened, and her eyes grew large. She whirled around to look at him, and he plastered a big smile on his face.

"No. N-not interested," Molly slurred.

"It looks like you're interested, doll. You've been teasing me with that backside of yours all night."

Molly shook her head to try and clear it. "N-no, I haven't. I'm dancing with my girls."

Molly looked around to see each of her girls dancing with other guys. Uh oh, not good.

"Come on, you little tease. Let's get out of here. Now!"

Molly could see his anger had bubbled to the surface and he grabbed for her, but she stepped back just in time. He lunged forward again and caught her arm in his hand. He pulled her roughly to him, and with a little more force and menace, he said, "Like I said—let's get out of here. You can play hard to get later."

Molly pushed against him, but he was stronger than her and not nearly as drunk. She pushed again and looked around at her girl-friends to get their attention. They were otherwise occupied. She pushed against him once more, but he didn't budge. Feeling nauseous and dizzy, she started to panic. Shit. Tears sprang to her eyes.

Abruptly, the man holding her arm jerked away. Molly blinked back the tears in her eyes to see Ryder hit the guy in the face.

"The lady said no. That means *no*, fuckface."

The jerk flew across the floor on his ass. Ryder looked at Molly; his jaw set tight.

"You okay?"

She was so relieved that tears started flowing from her eyes. She wiped the tears from her face and looked up just in time to feel strong warm arms come around her and pull her close.

"It's okay, Molly. I won't let anything happen to you." He held her tight for a few moments, letting her compose herself.

She felt good in his arms—soft and warm—her scent wafted up to his nostrils. She smelled heavenly, like a spring breeze and powder. She felt him nuzzle her hair, and she closed her eyes.

They were jostled as the guy lunged at them and pushed Ryder from behind. Before he could swing around, JT and Gunnar each had a hand on him and were dragging him back.

With his mouth close to her ear, Ryder said, "Hey, why don't I make sure you get home?"

She nodded and looked up at him as she finished wiping her eyes. Her head was swimming, and she felt unsteady. Suddenly her stomach lurched, and she ran for the front door. Ryder followed her outside just in time to see her throwing up alongside the building. The side of his mouth quirked up as he walked to where she hunched over, spilling her guts onto the parking lot. He stood just close enough that he would be available if she needed help, but he wanted to give her some privacy. He pulled a napkin out of his pocket. It had Rachel's phone number on it, but he didn't give a shit; he told her he wasn't interested, but she insisted on shoving it in his pocket anyway. When Molly lifted up her head, he walked over and handed it to her.

"Here you go. Can I get you some water or something?"

She took the napkin and wiped her mouth with it, unable to look at him. She had just humiliated herself. Great. Not only did he think she wasn't hot enough to date, now he wouldn't want to date her for sure.

"No, thanks. I'll be fine. I'll just go and see if the girls are ready to go."

Ryder stepped forward. "You said I could make sure you get home."

Molly looked at him for a long moment. Shit, her brain short-circuited when he was around. Well, why not, he already saw her throw up, how much worse could it get? She nodded and closed her eyes.

He put his arm around her shoulders. "My truck is over there," he said, pointing to his right. She had a hard time walking a straight line and put her arm around his waist to keep from falling. He chuckled to himself as he helped her into his truck and reached across her to fasten the seat belt. As he walked around to the driver's side of the truck, he glanced up at Molly through the windshield and saw her eyes closed.

"Hey! Wait a minute!"

Ryder looked up to see Tammy running toward him.

"Hey. Are you taking Molly home?"

Ryder nodded. "Yeah. She'll be fine. I won't hurt her."

Tammy smiled at him. "Didn't think you would. I have her purse."

Tammy held Molly's purse out to Ryder. He took it from her as he said thanks and turned to get in his truck.

"She really likes you. Don't you go hurting my girl," Tammy admonished.

Ryder glanced at Tammy a moment, then back at Molly. He smiled and nodded as he climbed into the truck, turned the key in the ignition and realized he didn't know where Molly lived. He looked back to ask Tammy, but she was gone. *Now what?* He *could* go digging around in her purse, but that wouldn't be right.

He drove to his place and carried Molly into his bedroom. She never woke up as he laid her on his bed and removed the heels from her feet.

"How the hell do women wear these things anyway? Geez," he whispered. He set them on the floor next to the bed along with her purse. He pulled the wastebasket close to the side of the bed in case she got sick in the middle of the night. He put a bottle of water and aspirin on the bedside table and then covered her with a blanket. Not being able to resist, he ran his hand across her forehead and then pulled his fingers through her hair. As he suspected, it was soft and supple.

Ryder leaned forward and kissed her forehead. "Goodnight, babe."

# 6

## OH GOD! THE MORNING AFTER

Molly opened her eyes and looked around. She didn't recognize anything in the room; she didn't remember this place at all. Her heart hammered, and her head was throbbing like crazy Her mouth felt awful. Yuck. She closed her eyes and tried to remember what had happened last night. Oh geez, that man on the dance floor. He'd grabbed her and was pulling her off the floor. Her heartbeat sped up. She sat up straight in a panic. What she saw was Ryder looking at her.

"Morning. How do you feel?"

Molly sat perfectly still. She was stunned. She was with Ryder? She looked down at her clothes; she was fully dressed. He was still wearing the clothes he had on last night. He was sitting in a chair at the end of the bed with his feet propped up on the footboard.

"Did you sleep there last night?"

He smiled. "Yeah. I wanted to be close in case you needed something. But I didn't want to freak you out or scare you by lying in bed next to you, so I slept here."

"Where's 'here'?" Molly was beginning to remember. Ryder punched that guy on the dance floor and walked her out. No, wait, she ran out and threw up. Shit, that's right. She puked in the parking lot in front of Ryder. *Just. Great.*

"I brought you to my house. You fell asleep before I could ask you where you live."

He watched her closely. He still thought she was gorgeous, even after waking up from a night of partying with her hair messed up from sleeping. He could imagine that's how it might look after he fucked her. Her blue eyes were staring warily at him. She licked her lips and rubbed her eyes.

"Oh."

"You didn't answer my question. How do you feel?"

Molly wrinkled her face. "My head hurts. My pride hurts. I'm embarrassed." She took a deep breath. "Mostly, I'm just embarrassed."

Ryder laughed. "I've been there; in fact, just last week, after my mom and dad's wedding."

He got up to place a notebook on top of the dresser, then turned and pointed out the bottle of water and aspirin he'd gotten for her.

"I brought you these in case you needed them. Can I get you anything else?"

Molly looked at the table and saw the water and aspirin. *Aww, now that was sweet of him.* She looked back up at him and smiled.

"No. Thank you for thinking of me...for taking care of me." Her voice was soft. Softer yet, she said, "I'm sorry if I ruined your date." She glanced down at her hands as they clutched the blanket.

He rubbed his hand over the back of his neck and rotated his head. He sat next to her legs on the bed. When she felt the bed dip and saw him sitting there, she looked up in surprise.

"You didn't ruin anything, and she wasn't my date. She'd walked up to me just before you walked into The Barn."

She reached over and grabbed the bottle of water. Her hands shook, and she had a hard time breaking open the seal. Their fingers brushed as he gently took the bottle from her to crack open the seal. He returned the bottle, and she swallowed down the aspirin with a long pull of water. She closed her eyes as the water hit her empty stomach.

"You should come in the kitchen and eat something quick before that aspirin hits your empty stomach. It might make you sick. Gunnar's cooking this morning. I think it's pancake day." He smiled.

Molly's eyes got huge. "Gunnar? You live with Gunnar?"

Ryder laughed. "And JT. I heard them both up a while ago. Actually, it's pretty early for both of them to be up on a Sunday, but neither of them had dates, so they were both home early last night. Right after we got home."

Molly covered her face with both hands. Oh. My. God. They were all going to think she and Ryder...well. Anyway. Now she was mortified. They would tell Joci, and she would think Molly was a slut. Crap. How the hell was she going to get out of this?

Taking a deep breath, Molly asked, "What time is it?"

He looked at his phone and back up at her. "Nine-fifteen."

She closed her eyes again. Shit.

"Hey, come on." Ryder got up and walked to the dresser. He grabbed a t-shirt and some sweatpants and tossed them on the bed next to her. "Throw these on and come on out and eat some breakfast. I'll take you home afterward."

"I'm *really* embarrassed now!" she softly said.

"What are you embarrassed about? They saw you last night. You were dancing and having a great time. They saw that bastard grab you and they were right behind me in case it got nasty. Lucky for that son-of-a-bitch, he walked away after they pulled him back and had words with him."

"But I spent the night here. They'll think..."

Ryder grinned. "They'll think I got lucky?"

Molly nodded.

"And the bastards will be jealous." Ryder laughed at the look on her face. "Don't worry; they like you, Molly. It'll be fine. Come on now, before your stomach gets upset."

Ryder stepped out into the hall and closed the door. She got up and pulled her dress off quickly and threw on the t-shirt and sweatpants. They had a tie string so she could tighten them up; she breathed a sigh of relief. She certainly wouldn't win any fashion awards, but at least she was warm and covered up. She left her shoes on the floor and walked out to the hallway. Ryder stood just outside the door. He grabbed her hand, and she looked up at him. He smiled and pointed to the door across the hall.

"Do you need to use the bathroom?"

She nodded and walked to the door Ryder had pointed to. She closed the door behind her and shut her eyes. She was so humiliated. Now she was going to have to walk into the kitchen and face JT and Gunnar, too. She used the toilet and moved to the sink to wash up. She looked into the mirror and groaned. She glanced around and saw washcloths folded in a basket on a shelf. A basket? In a home shared by three men? Sheesh. She took one and wet it in the sink and wiped at the dark makeup under her eyes to make herself look as presentable as possible. She rinsed her mouth and finger-brushed her teeth. It wasn't perfect, but it was all she had. When she finished, she opened the door and saw Ryder was waiting for her in the hall-way, just a few feet from the door. She was startled to see him.

He smiled. "I thought you would be uncomfortable walking into the kitchen by yourself. I hope you don't mind. Besides...I just got lucky, so we should be walking in together." He winked again, took her hand, and pulled her toward the kitchen.

She whispered, "If you'd really gotten lucky with me last night, we'd still be in bed." Ryder's steps faltered, and he turned to look at her. His face said he was debating whether or not to actually take her back to the bedroom and find out for sure.

His cock jumped into hyper-alert at the innuendo. His eyes bored into hers, and his nostrils flared. Shit, she already had his body going crazy for her. He liked the way he felt when she was around. When she smiled, his groin would sometimes tighten up to the point of pain. This woman was different.

They continued walking and rounded a corner that brought them into the kitchen. JT sat at the kitchen table with a cup of coffee and the newspaper. When he saw them, he smiled.

"Morning."

"Morning. Hope you're both hungry." Gunnar turned to look at them and then back at the bacon cooking on the stove.

"Morning," they said in unison.

"Do you want coffee, Molly?" She nodded and Ryder pointed her to a seat at the table, then walked to get them each a cup of coffee. He filled their cups and brought them to the table, returning to the counter to grab the sugar and creamer and set them on the table, as well. Once again, he grabbed the coffeepot and brought it over to refill his brothers' cups. He returned to the table and sat next to Molly.

∼

She watched with fascination as these guys took care of each other. Gunnar brought food to the table, and JT got up to help. As they filled their plates, Molly could no longer contain herself.

"So, how does this work? You take turns cooking?"

Ryder grinned. "Yeah. We take turns doing everything. This week it's Gunnar's turn to cook. It's my turn to do yard work. It's JT's turn to clean the house. We switch each week. That way, no one gets stuck doing all of one thing. We each do our own laundry. It works for us."

"Except I'm better at cooking," Gunnar said, a big smile growing on his face.

"Bullshit, Gunnar." JT looked at Molly with a devilish smile on his face.

"I make a mean omelet, and I am a master on the grill." He worked his eyebrows up and down and put a huge forkful of pancake in his mouth.

Ryder shot Molly a smug grin. He took a drink of his coffee and looked back toward her as he set his cup down on the table.

"They're both full of shit. I'm the one who knows his way around the kitchen. I spent a ton of time with my grandma growing up, and she taught me all sorts of cooking tips. I can cook the pants off these guys."

She giggled. "So which one of you guys put the washcloths in the basket in the bathroom?"

They chuckled, and Molly could feel herself begin to relax.

"That was Mom. She just couldn't help coming over and decorating and making things homey." JT smirked.

No one made a comment about her being there. No one said anything about her being drunk last night. She ate a few pancakes, and her tummy felt better. Her head felt better too. They made small talk during breakfast, and Molly felt comfortable with them. Ryder seemed very open and relaxed as well. He brought her into the conversation often, never leaving her out of any of it.

Gunnar said, "We're going to ride today. You guys coming?"

Ryder asked, "You going to call Mom and Dad?"

JT shook his head. "We talked about it last night. They haven't ridden since Mom's accident, so they want to ride for a bit. If it gets cold, they'll leave early. Dad's a little overprotective yet."

"That's an understatement," Gunnar said. "Do you ride, Molly?"

"No, I never have. It looks fun, though. I was envious of the riders at the Veteran's Ride."

R yder smiled at the memory of the Veteran's Ride. "Yeah. It's a great feeling to ride. The wind hits your face, and you're floating along the road alone with your thoughts."

"If you have any." JT chuckled.

"Fuck you, JT," Ryder chuckled. Gunnar laughed.

"You said your mom and dad are going? Isn't she afraid after her accident?"

Gunnar replied, "Nah. Mom's not scared. But she probably won't ever be able to drive her own bike again. Her shoulder and arm are pretty banged up. There are pins in her arm, and the doctors told her she would probably have trouble being able to hold her arm out fully in front of her. It's painful if she holds it out in front for any length of time. She's not happy about having to give it up, but Dad loves her riding on the back with him, so she'll still be able to ride a lot."

Ryder looked at his brothers. "What happened to Mom wasn't her fault. But if you ride, chances are one day you may have an accident.

No different than driving a car. There are so many elements out there: weather, other drivers, road conditions, animals running into the road—all of it. But the days that are good are great."

"Wow. She's fortunate she wasn't hurt worse. I saw the pictures of her bike after the accident. It was awful."

The boys nodded.

"What's going to happen to LuAnn?" Molly asked.

Gunnar took a deep breath. "There'll probably be a trial. We're just hoping when they offer her a plea deal that she'll take it so Mom doesn't have to go through one. But LuAnn's pretty selfish and thinking of someone else isn't likely to happen. She's asked twice if Dad would come and talk to her, but he's refused. He'll go if she agrees to take the deal. He doesn't want Mom to go through a trial after all she's been through." He shrugged. "We'll see what happens. Should know in a month or so."

Molly nodded. She'd heard a lot of talk at the wedding, and that was the consensus, but she didn't want to ask questions and seem nosy.

"You should go on a ride with us today," Gunnar said.

Ryder glanced at her, his green eyes boring into hers, willing her to say yes.

"Umm, I don't know." Molly flicked her eyes to Gunnar's and then back to Ryder.

"I'm a good driver. I won't let anything happen to you. Come on and try something new," he urged.

She looked at Ryder and swallowed the lump in her throat. He was asking her out—finally. When he looked into her eyes and was this close to her, she couldn't seem to think clearly. And he still smelled so good, but she wasn't sure if it was the shirt she was wearing or him.

She smiled softly. "Okay." Her cheeks tinted pink, and she glanced at her coffee cup.

~

He let out a breath. Whew, that wasn't so bad. She was so beautiful, her eyes were shining, and he could tell she was feeling better as the color came back to her cheeks. She smiled more, too. He wanted to see her smile all the time. Seeing her in his clothes made him feel all sorts of crazy things. He kept imagining pulling them off of her. That dress she was wearing last night revealed what a fabulous body she had, but he wanted to see all of it.

"Excellent. Then it's settled. I'll call Mom and let her know; she'll be thrilled. Dress warm; it's a little cool out today." Gunnar continued talking, with no one else able to get a word in.

When they finished breakfast, Ryder took Molly's hand and pulled her back to the bedroom to grab her dress and shoes. She hesitated and turned to look at him.

"I should change back into my dress and give you your clothes back." Her voice was soft.

"Why don't you leave them on? It's a little cool outside, and you might be happy to have something warmer on. In fact, if you need a jacket, I have an extra one you can wear today."

"Thank you." She smiled brightly, and he thought his heart would bust right out of his chest. He couldn't wait to let out a howl in celebration of the fact that he would be with her all day.

He walked to his closet and pulled out a black leather jacket loaded with zippers and studs. He held it open for Molly to slide her arms in. As he lifted it to her shoulders, his knuckles brushed the back of her neck. She shivered at the contact and his throat instantly dried up; his heartbeat picked up and his stomach flipped over.

Masking his emotions, he said, "See, you were cold. Good thing I have an old jacket for you."

~

She nodded. No need in telling him it wasn't the temperature of the room that made her shiver. The jacket felt heavy and warm, and as she bent her head to zip it up, a puff of air lifted to her nostrils, and she smelled...Ryder—the scent she remembered from the wedding, the scent in his shirt, the scent that was permanently imprinted on her brain. Another shiver ran down her body and landed in her core, creating an ache between her legs.

"There. Now my house is programmed into your GPS. See?" Molly smiled as she pointed to the GPS on his console.

"Thanks. Now I'll be able to come back to your place again." He stared into her eyes and she fell into the depths of the green vision before her, like fresh spring grass surrounded by the deeper tones of pine trees. It was impossible not to stare at them; they were so unusual. Then he smiled at her—those lips, so soft and full, held promises of so much more.

She stared for a beat, but the lump in her throat at the look on his face and the innuendo in his comment made impressive words impossible. All she could manage was, "Awesome."

On the ride to her place, she stared out the window, trying to sort through her thoughts and emotions. Last night she'd been jealous, even though she had no right to be. This morning, just seeing him at home in his element, made her want to spend more time with him. She liked Joci so much, and she assumed Joci's family would be like her, and her boys were great—this one in particular. As soon as he realized what kind of person she was, he would run for the hills, and that might hurt. She was starting to like him. A lot.

"What are you thinking about?"

She turned to see Ryder looking at her. He glanced back to the road and then shot her another quick look. When she hesitated, he raised an eyebrow in question.

She smiled softly. "You know, I don't have to go along today. I know you said you wanted me to join you, but it's a family day for you, and I don't want to barge in."

He looked at the road again and then back at Molly.

"You need to stop worrying about that. You already know my family, and you'll love riding. It gets in your blood. And," she saw him swallow, "I *want* you to come with us." He let out a deep breath.

She sucked in hers. "Okay. I'm excited to go. I'll be like a real biker bitch or something." She laughed as she watched her words roll around his brain.

He burst out laughing. Oh. My. God. When he laughed, he was beautiful, simply beautiful. And, damn, it made her insides clench and moisten. His features were perfect—a strong jaw, full lips, beautiful skin. Gawd, he is something special.

Molly smiled and blew out a deep breath. "Did you think about asking me out at the wedding?"

He looked at her again. He swallowed and then nodded.

"Thank God." It came out before she could keep it from tumbling out of her mouth. She blushed and threw her hands up over her mouth as he glanced at her, surprise clear in his eyes.

He raised his brows, and she giggled—probably nerves. "I thought you weren't interested."

He chuckled. "Well, that was before I knew you couldn't hold your liquor."

She groaned. "Sorry we had to get together after I puked. How humiliating. I still can't believe I let myself get so bad."

"Why did you?" One corner of his perfect mouth hitched up.

She grinned. "You need your ego stroked, Ryder?"

"No. Why did you, Molly?"

She took a deep breath and let it out slowly. "I was jealous."

He raised an eyebrow. "That so? What were you jealous of?"

He pulled into Molly's driveway and put the truck in park.

"Forget it, Ryder. I'm not stroking your ego anymore. Do you want to come in and wait for me to change or come back?"

He smiled. She was jealous, huh? "I'll come back and get you with the bike. We'll need to be at Mom and Dad's in an hour. I'll be back in about fifty minutes or so."

She opened the door of his truck and jumped out. She was still wearing the clothes he loaned her and her heels from last night. She turned to tell him she would get his clothes back to him, but when she looked in the truck, he'd gotten out and had walked around the side to her. His eyebrows were pinched together. She cocked her head when she saw his face pinched up.

"You make it hard for me to mind my manners when you don't let me open your door. My grandma would kick my ass if she thought I wasn't a gentleman. Mom too."

She giggled. "Sorry. I'm not used to anyone being gentlemanly toward me."

He furrowed his brow again and gently bowed in front of her. He stood and held his arm out. She placed her arm through his as they walked to her front door, both of them laughing at his feigned gallantry.

# 7

# RIDING IN THE FALL

R yder picked Molly up for their ride a few minutes before noon. She had quickly showered and blown her hair dry. Good thing it was short and dried quickly. She put a black bandana over her hair like she'd seen the women do at the Veteran's Ride, to keep her hair from blowing all over. She applied a small amount of makeup and some lip gloss and threw on a pair of jeans and an army green wrap sweater with a white camisole underneath. She wore army green suede shoe-boots as well, and she still had Ryder's leather jacket.

The deep rumble of his motorcycle drew her attention to the window, and she watched as he pulled into her driveway. And damn, the way he looked on his bike—it was swoon worthy. Well, if you were a swooner, and she wasn't.

She left the bathroom and headed to the front door just as he knocked. Taking a deep breath, she pulled it open. She flushed as she took him in. He wore jeans that hugged his legs and his, um...front, perfectly. The unzipped black leather jacket similar to the one she wore gave him a 'badass' look. His light green shirt highlighted the color of his eyes, and the shirt cuffs peeked out from under the sleeves of his leather. His spiky hair looked perfect, even after making the short ride over from his place— _mouthwateringly delicious. A shiver ran the length of her body, and her nipples puckered tight.

His voice raspy, he said, "You look beautiful, Molly."

She blinked, taking in what he just said. "You look amazing yourself, Ryder. Wow." She sighed. Gawd, she wasn't a sigher.

He blushed and cleared his throat. "You ready?"

She nodded. "Um, thank you for letting me wear your jacket today. I don't have any riding clothes."

"You look much better in it than I ever did." He blushed all the way to the tips of his ears.

She softly smiled as she walked out and closed her front door. "Oh, wait. I want to bring my tablet and show your mom some of the wedding pictures. I know she'll see them tomorrow, but I thought she might like to take a peek if we have any time today. Is that okay?"

"Of course. She'll be thrilled. Thanks for thinking of her."

She ran back into the house to grab her tablet and tossed it into her big bag. He smiled as she walked back outside. She was feeling giddy knowing she was about to go riding with Ryder. She couldn't wait to call Tammy and tell her!

Ryder took her bag. "I can put this in one of the side bags if you'd like. It'll get heavy carrying it."

She grinned. His stomach rolled, and his cock throbbed when he looked at her. That smile of hers was what he'd been thinking about this whole week. Her perfect teeth, full lips, and that body. Jesus. He was going to have a hard-on all damn day.

He strode to the bike and pulled open one of the side bags. He pulled out a pair of gloves and handed them to her.

"It'll be a little cold while we ride. That's the best part of riding in the fall. You feel the crisp air and get a little chilled. When we stop, we can have hot chocolate or tea and warm up. After the ride today, we'll go to Mom and Dad's house for chili If you don't have supper plans."

"That sounds delicious."

"Molly...I..." Ryder turned, shaking his head and started to get on his bike. He stopped and looked at her. Fuck it. He wanted to kiss her. He leaned forward before he lost his nerve and touched his lips to hers. She sighed. The hunger he had felt all week prompted him to kiss her thoroughly. He reached out and cupped the back of her head, adding pressure to the kiss. He licked her lips, and she opened her mouth, allowing him access. He slipped his tongue into her mouth and caught her second sigh. He felt her grab his jacket on each side and hang on. He ended the kiss with a little nip on her bottom lip. When he pulled his head back, he looked into her incredible blue eyes.

"I've wanted to do that for a long time."

She sounded breathless. "Me too."

His full-blown smile stretched across his face. She looked at him and blinked before uttering, "Oh."

He turned and threw his leg over his bike, feeling rather proud of himself.

"Your bike is awesome."

He looked back at her and saw her eyes stroking the fenders of his bike. Yep, hard-on. All day. She placed her hands tentatively on his shoulders and threw her leg over the seat. As soon as she sat down, she gripped his jacket on the sides and sat stiff as a board.

He chuckled and reached back for her hands and pulled them forward and around his waist. "Hang on to me tight. Okay?"

"Okay."

"Don't let your legs touch the pipes." He pointed to her right side. "Until you get used to the feel of the bike and the leaning when I turn into any corner, look in the direction I'm turning. If you're comfortable, you can rest your chin on the shoulder in the direction we're turning. Yeah?"

"Um, yeah."

"If you try to pull me out of the corner, it could cause us issues. Okay?"

"Okay."

~

Holy shit, there was a lot to this whole riding thing. Her heart began beating out a dance rhythm as Ryder started his bike, and off they went. The rumble of the bike shot through her body, the thumping of the motor in her chest and the vibration between her legs. The power when he rolled on the throttle made her spine tingle; the thrill of the wind in her hair and brushing her face was invigorating, and she felt...free.

They arrived at Jeremiah and Joci's house about ten minutes later. A lot of the family was already there and standing outside talking. Joci smiled and waved when they pulled up. Molly waved in response. As soon as he pulled to a stop, she climbed off the bike and waited for Ryder. Once he put the kickstand down and climbed off, he grabbed her hand and walked with her to his family. She watched as he kissed his mom, hugged his dad, and said hello to everyone else. "You all remember Molly from the wedding?"

"Of course. Happy you could join us today, Molly," Staci replied.

"Thank you; I'm excited. Oh, Joci. I brought my tablet with the pictures on it. I know we're meeting tomorrow to look at them in detail, but in case you wanted a sneak peek, I brought them today."

Joci squealed. "I can't wait to see them. We're still waiting for Bryce and Angie. Can we take a quick peek now?"

"Of course." Molly quickly walked back to Ryder's bike for her tablet. As she returned to the group, she turned it on. Joci patted the top of the tour pack on Jeremiah's bike and she set it up and started the picture show as everyone oohed and aahed over the pictures.

Jeremiah wrapped his arms around Joci from behind and rested his chin on the top of her head as they looked at them. They were beaming. When the slideshow stopped, Joci hugged Molly.

"Thank you for bringing this, Molly. They turned out fantastic. I can't wait to take a longer look at them. You'll have to do the slideshow again when Angie gets here. She'll want to see."

"No problem. We can show it as many times as you want to see it." She beamed at bringing something to the table. It was a bit intimidating joining a whole family at once during an activity they loved and had shared often. Her nerves settled, and her stomach ceased its churning.

Bryce and Angie pulled up, and they watched the slideshow again. When it was finished, she folded up the cover to her tablet and began walking back to the bike to put it away. She had tucked it back in the side bag and stood up. Seeing that Ryder had followed her, the smile stretched across her face.

"Thank you for bringing that for my mom. You just made her day. Did you see her smile?"

She nodded and looked over to see Joci smiling at and hugging Jeremiah.

"She's great, you know? I liked her from the first moment I met her. I know she had a hard life before, and I'm thrilled beyond words that her life is so good now. And you're welcome, but you don't have to thank me. I was excited to be asked to take their wedding pictures. I'm so happy to be able to make her smile."

Ryder looked over at his mom and dad. "Yeah, she's great. My dad's never been so happy. When they found out she was pregnant—well, he was over the moon. She's treated JT and me with so much respect and given us more love in such a short time than our biological mother ever has. We both love her a lot."

Jeremiah whistled, indicating it was time to saddle up and ride. They climbed on the bike and followed JT and Gunnar, who would be leading today. They pulled out of the driveway and headed toward Manitowoc on the back roads.

Molly was amazed at the ride. She felt safe with Ryder, never nervous or scared in any way. They rode in the middle of the pack with Joci and Jeremiah beside them. Every once in a while Joci would look over and smile at her, and it made her feel like she belonged in this group. A few times throughout the day, Ryder took his left hand off the handlebars and laid it on Molly's knee. Each time he did, it gave her a bigger thrill than the time before. Her warm and fuzzy emotions were beginning to settle between her legs.

She enjoyed watching the beautiful scenery pass by as they rode along the back roads. She could see the appeal to riding—watching the passing houses and farms, seeing the animals, feeling the wind dance across her face—it was so freeing. The air was chilly, but not biting cold. Rather, it was refreshing and made her feel more alive than she had ever felt before. Even though they were in a group while on the bike, you were virtually alone with your thoughts. As they rode through a couple of small towns, some of the people would stop to look at the bikes while others would point and wave like they knew them.

While they ate pizza at The Iron Buffalo, some drank hot chocolate to warm up from the cold. Molly found she was comfortable standing around talking with everyone. Joci and Jeremiah regaled them with stories of their honeymoon and some of the things they saw. Ryder stayed close and always made sure she was taken care of.

Ryder and Molly stood with Gunnar and Angie when Joci approached. "Molly, I was going to talk to you about this tomorrow, but if you're available next weekend, I'd like to have you take pictures at the build we're doing for Danny Schaefer. He's the veteran receiving the bulk of the donations from the Veteran's Ride. Are you interested? I want them for the video."

"Oh, that would be fabulous. Yes, I would love to participate in the build. I don't have anything on my calendar for the whole weekend if you need me. Thanks, Joci."

Joci smiled. "Thank *you*. It'll be fun. We'll have food and beverage tables set up in the yard, and I plan to interview Danny as well for the end of the video."

"That's really cool; great way to end the video."

After they had eaten, they saddled back up and hit the road before dark settled in.

Around four forty-five they pulled into Joci and Jeremiah's driveway. "Are you okay going in without me, Molly?" Ryder asked. "I want to run the bike home and bring the truck back; otherwise, the ride home will be bitter cold."

"I'm fine, go on ahead. I'll help your mom get things ready."

Walking into the house with Gunnar and JT, Molly removed her jacket and handed it to Gunnar's waiting hands.

"Mom's in the kitchen, go on in." He nodded toward the back of the house.

The tasty aroma of chili and freshly baking buns in the oven made Molly's mouth water. Joci smiled up at her and handed her a stack of bowls.

"Can you set these on the table and then help with shredding the cheese?"

Relieved she would not be in the way, she did as Joci asked, happy to be ensconced in this family and watching the bustle going on around her as the men grabbed beers from the fridge and Jeremiah stole spoons of chili from the pot and Joci smacking him on the butt.

As they ate, Molly said, "Joci, this apple pie is the best I've ever eaten."

Gunnar smirked. "That's where I got my great pancake recipe. Molly loved my pancakes this morning, Mom."

Molly was horrified that he would say anything. She didn't want Joci knowing she'd spent the night at their place last night. Her face flamed a bright red, and she looked at Gunnar with eyes the size of saucers. She heard JT chuckle. He just smiled at her as she immediately darted her eyes to his. Molly braved a look at Joci, who grinned at her.

"She also likes the little basket in the bathroom with the towels in it." Now it was JT's turn to tease her.

Molly's eyes squinted as she looked at Gunnar. Oh, he so started this!

"Really? You're going there?"

Gunnar looked up at the ceiling, probably doing a quick scan through his brain of anything she might have on him. He must have felt safe because his grin turned into a smile, and he nodded and said, "Yup!"

Molly gave her head a nod, and said, "Paybacks are a bitch, Gunnar. Just sayin'."

She shot JT a look as he chuckled. She took a few calming breaths, willing her face to return to a normal color.

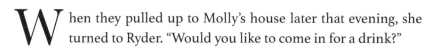

W hen they pulled up to Molly's house later that evening, she turned to Ryder. "Would you like to come in for a drink?"

He glanced at her and nodded. He'd been working up in his mind how they would say goodnight. He hoped it would be together or at least with plans for another date.

"I can make hot chocolate, if you'd like."

"That would be great."

She put the milk on the stove on a low heat. "How about a tour of the house? It won't take long." She giggled.

He nodded, trying to fight off the nerves crawling through his body. "Yeah, thanks."

She smiled and walked through the kitchen to a hallway. When she stepped past him, he caught a whiff of her perfume. She smelled like cinnamon and something completely edible. "I've rented this house for five years now. The landlord is an older man, and we have a verbal agreement that when he's ready to sell, I can buy it. It's a bit old, but I love the woodwork and arched doorways. I've spent a ton of time painting and fixing it up." She turned to a room that seemed to serve as an office. "Sometimes the money has been tight, so I do little things when I can. Freelancing means that sometimes I don't have a steady income. But the work has been coming more frequently now, so hopefully purchasing it won't be an enormous burden. I just love this neighborhood."

They stepped back into the kitchen, and he watched as she finished mixing the cocoa into the pan of warm milk and poured them each a cup. She handed him a cup and motioned with her hand to the little kitchen table by the sliding glass doors.

As they sat, he asked, "What do you do when you're not taking pictures, Molly?"

She smiled. "I love to read books. I work in my yard. I spend time with my friends. What do you like to do?"

He chuckled. "My brothers and I always find something to do. We work out in the basement, shoot pool, throw the football around. We spend time with my parents and grandparents. Of course, we ride a lot in the summer. What about your parents or siblings?"

She scrunched her pretty face briefly. "I don't have any siblings. My mother's in a nursing home not far from here."

"Sorry, that sucks. Do you see her much?"

"She doesn't really know who I am. I used to go more often, but it makes me so sad that I only make myself go about once a month now."

He looked into her eyes when she spoke. Something just happened there; a sadness crept in. "What about your father?"

"Did you need more hot chocolate?" Molly asked, evading his question. "How about something to eat? I know it's cold outside, but I have ice cream."

He leaned back in his chair; she didn't want to talk about her father, so he would let it go for now. But this girl was something. Self-sufficient, sweet and yet, sad. He suspected there were layers to uncover, and he wanted to be the one to peel them away.

He looked into her eyes. "I better go," he said. "Work tomorrow. You'll be taking pictures of the build next weekend. I have a ton of work to do this week leading up to that, but can we get together afterward on Saturday night?"

"I would like that very much. I'll see you then."

She walked him to the door where he turned and quickly kissed her before he lost his nerve. His lips gently slid over hers; his hands held her face, his breathing accelerated, lost in the taste of her. He stepped away and kissed the tip of her nose, then turned and walked out the door.

# 8

## DANNY SCHAEFER

The week flew by in a blur. Molly spent Monday with Joci and Jeremiah going over the pictures in greater detail. They discussed the pictures they wanted hard copies of and the ones they wanted for gift giving. Molly gave Joci all of the digital pictures, then presented her idea of using the boys in the shop's advertising.

"I want to show you something else. Look at the pictures of your sons. The three of them together are *hot!*" Molly's face flamed bright red as she quickly looked down at the picture of them. "I think you could really do some fabulous promotions using the guys on posters and ads. Put them in some biker gear and you'll have the women lining up to get in the doors. When the women come, the men will follow."

"You're right about that, Molly. Not that I want to pimp the boys out, but looking at them all together like that, I can see the potential. Jeremiah, what do you think?"

"I think you ladies are on to something. Let's use the clothing we sell here and put them in front of our bikes and see what kind of response we get."

"Okay. I'll set it up with you after we speak with the boys. For now, we have a build from the Veteran's Ride this weekend."

"I'm excited to be a part of that. Thank you again." Molly's tummy flitted with excitement at the thought of bringing a marketing idea to Joci and Jeremiah. It didn't hurt that she'd get to spend more time with Ryder. After spending the day with him on Sunday, she wanted to spend more time with him. As men went, he came from a great family. He hadn't been in any legal trouble over the years, or Joci would have mentioned that. He was incredibly attractive and genuinely a nice man. She could definitely do worse.

R yder felt light on his feet all week. He thought the ride on Sunday had gone well. He liked having Molly on the back of his bike. He just liked being around her—period. It was a bonus that his parents liked her, too. She was smart, talented, and independent and yet, there was something about her—she was vulnerable in a way and she had things that were painful in her past. She didn't want to talk about her father, that was for sure. She was alone in this world, or so it seemed, except for her friends. More than ever Ryder felt lucky as hell. He had a big loving family to lean on. And he wanted to make sure Molly had them, too. Now that he had gotten to spend some time with her, he realized maybe his mom was right—he would move heaven and earth to be with her and to make her happy.

Ryder walked through the shop and found his dad working on his bike. He walked over to see what he was doing; he didn't work on the bikes much anymore.

"Hey Dad, what's up?"

"Hi, son. I'm working on a backrest for your mom. She said it was a bit uncomfortable the other day. I want to tilt it out on the bottom. Can you hold this?"

Ryder leaned forward and pulled the bottom of the backrest out while his dad tightened the screws in the back.

"Can I talk to you about something?"

"Ryder, you can always talk to me. You know that."

He swallowed. "I like Molly. A lot."

"Mm-hm. We could see that."

"Yeah, well, I don't want to fuck up."

Jeremiah stood and looked at him. Setting his wrench down on the top of the bike lift, he grabbed a rag and wiped his hands.

"I assume there's a question coming."

"Yeah. Well, I don't want to hurt your feelings, but when JT and I were growing up, you didn't really have girlfriends. We...I don't know what to do. I mean, I want to be with her and spend time with her, but it's just always been us. You know?"

Jeremiah's lips formed a straight line as he held Ryder's gaze. He nodded once and walked around the bike and stood in front of him.

"I'm sorry. I guess I didn't teach you boys how to be a good boyfriend. Is that what you're worried about?"

"Yeah. I mean, I'm not blaming you, I just...until Mom, we didn't have women around. Am I supposed to do something different? How did you know what to do when you met Mom?"

Taking a deep breath, Jeremiah slipped his fingers in his front pockets. "I didn't know either, Ryder. I waited an eternity to press the issue with Joci. I knew she was scared, and I didn't want to scare her away, so I dragged my feet until I thought I would go out of my mind. I finally just told her I wanted to be with her, and I knew she wanted to be with me, and that's the way it was going to be. Not exactly romantic or smooth, but I knew I couldn't wait any longer."

He nodded. "I remember what a crab ass you were back then," he teased, and his dad laughed.

"Well, so I guess we all learn as we go along. I guess you need to ask her out, spend time with her. Ask her what she likes and what she wants to do and don't waste a lot of time. If you know you want to be with her, take a page from my book and don't wait forever. Simple. The rest will come."

～

"Come with me, Tammy. I can take some 'before' pictures and then we can go out and grab a bite to eat. We can call Cara and Suzie and ask them to meet us." Molly packed her camera in her bag, checked her lenses and closed the case. Holding her phone to her ear, she smiled when Tammy agreed.

"Sounds good. I'll be over in about half an hour. This should be fun."

Tammy walked into Molly's living room and called out. "I'm here." Flipping her long dark hair over her shoulder, she sat on the sofa and grabbed a magazine from the coffee table and began flipping through a few pages.

Molly walked from the back of the house, carrying her camera bags. She set them down and said. "Are you ready?"

"You need magazines here besides photography magazines. What about some juicy gossip rags or something?"

"I don't have the time or the inclination to pay for that junk." She grabbed her keys from the counter and picked up her bags. "Come on Tam, I'll drive."

Molly and Tammy walked around the outside of Danny Schaefer's house. Tomorrow, the contractor and the crew that Rolling Thunder put together would be adding an addition to his house. Molly wanted before pictures so a photo montage could be put together for the Veteran's Ride DVDs that Joci was pulling together. They would be sold for ten bucks each to raise additional money for next year. It was a great cause, and it was a labor of love for Jeremiah.

The sun hung low in the sky, and the lighting was phenomenal. She captured the sun setting and the light peeking through the trees in Danny's yard. The summer flowers had long since died, but the fall mums, in burgundy and dark orange, as well as different varieties of kale were so lovely. She stopped taking pictures of the house long enough to snap a few flower pictures with the setting sun in the background. Some of these shots were destined to make great screen savers. She lie on the ground on her belly, to get a close-up shot of the flowers.

"Can I help you?"

She spun her head around to see a handsome man, leaning on crutches, looking at her from the front door. At a closer glance, she saw that he had a leg missing from the knee down. She stood up, hung her camera around her neck, and walked over to him.

"Hi, I'm Molly. I'm not sure if you remember me from the Veteran's Ride. This is my friend, Tammy. I'm the photographer hired to take pictures of the build tomorrow. I wanted to snap some before pictures and thought I would do it today in case I didn't get here before the workers do in the morning." She brushed dead leaves from the front of her blouse. "I'm sorry if I bothered you."

Molly watched him closely. He looked annoyed and stiff, and who could blame him? He didn't know who she was or what she was doing wandering around on his property.

"You think they're going to trample on my flowers?" he asked evenly.

She looked into his dark brown eyes—they were sad but nice to look at.

Her voice shook, as she replied, "No. Sorry, I walked through your flowers. They're so beautiful with the sun setting...I couldn't help myself." Lowering her voice, she said, "Sorry. I shouldn't have."

Danny's shoulders relaxed a little. "May I see?"

He flicked his gaze to Tammy, a soft smile creasing his face. Molly pulled her camera up and turned it on. She hit a few buttons and brought up the pictures she'd been taking. She smiled at Danny and turned the camera around so he could see them.

"You can scroll through the pictures by pushing this button."

She pointed to the button Danny needed to touch to move through the pictures. He leaned into his crutches and scrolled through the photos. He smiled a few times and looked up at Molly and Tammy.

"You have a good eye for this. I guess I haven't taken the time to enjoy those flowers. My mom planted them to make my house feel cheery or something." He scrubbed a hand along his jaw.

He grew quiet, and the silence stretched. Both women looked at him and wondered what to do next. He cleared his throat.

"Name's Danny. Would you like to come in and take before pictures of the inside?"

Molly raised her eyebrows and smiled. She looked back at Tammy, who nodded.

"We don't want to put you out, but it *would* be nice to get some before pictures of the house on the inside. Thank you."

He turned and walked into the house, leaving Molly and Tammy to follow. They walked in behind him and closed the door.

He pointed toward the wall on the west side of the house. "They're going to knock that wall out and put the addition there."

Molly walked over and began taking pictures of the room—her camera's shutter the only sound filling the silence.

"I *do* remember you. I thought you looked familiar, but I couldn't place where I'd seen you," Danny offered.

Tammy observed him as he began to relax. His hair was short, military style and sandy brown in color. He wore a day's worth of growth on his jaw which gave him a rugged, sexy look. His body was thin and ripped...hot. As if he could tell she was looking at him, he turned his gaze toward her. Their eyes met for a few beats, then she blushed and looked down. He chuckled.

"How does this happen, Danny? Will you have to go and stay somewhere else for a while or can you stay here?" Molly asked.

He turned toward Molly. "I can stay here. They'll frame the addition up first. They'll put the windows in and insulate, and then knock the wall out to allow the access. I have the plans on the table in the dining room if you want to see them."

Both women nodded and Danny walked them into the dining room. The plans lay on the modest square table, spread out, but neatly lined up together. Each of the eight chairs was pushed in tightly to allow for a portion of the plans to drape across the top of them. As they bowed their heads to look at the plans, he pointed out where they were standing and where the additional bedroom and bathroom would be. Molly immediately started snapping pictures of the plans —some up close, some from farther away. She snapped pictures of Danny and Tammy looking at the plans. She walked around and snapped pictures of the living room from this view. The constant click of her camera once more the only sound that was heard.

"Does she always do that?" he asked, in a lowered voice to Tammy.

Tammy smirked. "Yeah. It's her thing. You'll get used to her. She does have a good eye, and she just loves this stuff."

Molly heard them and blushed. "I'll make sure you get the digitals. You can do what you like with them, but it'll be pretty cool to see the before and after. Sometimes after a while, you forget what things looked like before." She moved to stand before the windows facing the front of the house. "I've painted and worked on my house—not to this degree—but months and years later when I come across the pictures, I'm still amazed at what it looked like before. It's what hooked me on photography in the first place. It's a beautiful way to memorialize the past."

Danny nodded. "Yeah, I was just looking at pictures of myself graduating from boot camp. Back when I had two legs. Kind of bittersweet."

Tammy looked at Danny. "Sometimes it can be. We can't always control it, but change happens every day. By the way, thank you for your service. It's appreciated more than you'll ever know." She smiled at him.

Danny nodded but continued holding her gaze.

She said. "Hey, we're going to head out and grab a bite to eat. Would you like to join us?"

He looked into Tammy's beautiful brown eyes. She was petite with long, sandy-brown hair, and she was *hot*. He hadn't dated since he'd lost his leg. He honestly didn't think any woman would want to have anything to do with him with only one leg. But...Tammy seemed interested.

He swallowed. "Nah. Thanks, but I think this'll be a full weekend. I have a few things to do around here before tomorrow." He watched as the smile faded from her lips. "I appreciate the offer."

She nodded. "If you change your mind, we're going to Micki's in De Pere. Please feel free to stop in. I'll buy you a beer." Tammy flashed her brightest smile. He swallowed again and cocked his head toward her.

They left Danny's house and headed to Micki's.

"So? What did you think?" Tammy looked at Molly, a huge grin on her face.

"About?"

"About Danny. Pretty hot, isn't he?"

Molly laughed. "Do you have a crush on Danny? You *so* have to come to the build tomorrow. You can help me out by moving my stuff around, and you can see him again. I think Joci and her sisters-in-law are bringing food and helping out where needed as well. Jeremiah won't let her do much, so if nothing else, you can talk to her so she doesn't get bored."

"Okay." She opened the car door to jump out. "He seems sad... But did you see the arms on him? His body? I bet he works out like crazy. He looks delicious." She fanned herself with her hand as they laughed and entered the bar. They ate as their friends wandered in to join them and the conversation flowed as they caught up on last weekend, and Molly told them about her night at Ryder's and the next day going for a bike ride with the group.

"There...see? You fretted over nothing, and he was into you all the time, just shy."

"Well, I haven't heard from him all week. He said he had a busy week, but I hoped for a call at least. Besides, I don't want to be like my mom. So, I'm going to sit back and wait and see what happens. We do have a date tomorrow night."

"God, Molly. Stop saying that. You're nothing like your mom. Your mom was weak and needed someone with her all the time. You're nothing like that. And the rest was not your fault. Stop thinking that way."

"In my head, I know this. But I never want to be like that." Molly popped a french fry in her mouth.

Cara patted Molly's hand. "Darlin', you're *nothing* like your mom. Now...to the important stuff. I want to see pictures of these hot guys you two are mooning over. Gimme."

Molly laughed as she pulled out her camera to show the girls the pictures she had taken of Danny and Ryder.

# 9

## THE VETERAN'S BUILD

Saturday morning came early. Pulling into Danny's driveway with a steaming cup of coffee, the boys each looked at the yard to see the activity had already begun at six-thirty in the morning. Due to the neighborhood covenants, power tools and hammering wouldn't start until eight o'clock, but preliminaries and unloading were in progress at the moment.

"Okay, let's get rolling." Gunnar jumped out of the driver's seat and grabbed his tool belt from the back seat. Ryder and JT did the same on the other side. They had decided to ride together to keep the number of vehicles down to a minimum. They made their way over to Jeremiah, who was speaking with the Steve, the contractor, about the day's events.

"Hey, Dad."

"Hi, guys. Steve, these are my sons: JT, Ryder, and Gunnar. Boys, you remember Steve? We were just discussing the events for today."

Just then, Danny walked out of his house. He was wearing a prosthetic leg today, covered up by his jeans. If it weren't for a slight limp, you wouldn't know anything was different about him. He stepped up to Jeremiah and gave him a hug.

"I don't know how to thank you, Dog. I'm overwhelmed, actually."

Jeremiah shook his head. "No need to thank me, Danny. Just enjoy your home and we'll be good."

"Hey guys, how are you today? Thanks for helping on this." Danny looked at the boys.

"Happy to help, Danny," JT said as he shook Danny's hand. Each, in turn, greeted Danny then turned to Jeremiah to see what they needed to start with. Danny looked over and saw some guys walking with boards over by the flowers.

"Can we ask the guys to be careful by the flower beds?" They turned their heads in the direction Danny was looking.

"I'll remind them that we aren't destroying anything, just making it better," Jeremiah replied, smiling.

"Good. That hot little photographer was here yesterday taking pictures, and she liked my flowers. I'll sic her and her sexy little friend on anyone who smashes them."

Ryder stiffened at the comment. Molly? Molly had been here yesterday? Did she know Danny? He called her hot. *What the fuck?* Gunnar and JT looked at Ryder, brows raised. Danny noticed it too.

Danny pointed his chin at Ryder. "She yours?"

Ryder's brows furrowed.

"What?"

"The hot photographer. Little gal with dark hair and startling blue eyes—Molly, I think. She yours? Everyone just looked at you when I mentioned her, and if you clench your jaw any tighter, you'll break a tooth."

Jeremiah interrupted, "They're dating, Danny."

Danny nodded and started to say something, but they were interrupted by Bryce, Angie, Dayton, and Staci.

"Morning everyone. Nice to see you, Danny. Ready for all of this?" Bryce asked, smiling.

"Yeah. I'm ready." Danny glanced at Ryder and turned to walk over to the table that was set up outside where the plans had been laid out.

Jeremiah tapped Ryder's shoulder. "You good? I don't want problems today. If you have issues, I would rather we work them out now."

"No, I'm good. I was just surprised that Molly was here yesterday; I didn't know she was coming."

"Well, if you don't fucking call her, you aren't going to know what she's doing and where she is, are you?" Gunnar sniped. "If you want Molly, you're going to have to show her that. You can't be mad that she was here—or anywhere, for that matter—if you don't show her you're interested."

"Fuck you, Gunnar." Ryder stormed off. Right now, he needed to do something physical to get rid of this frustration. Sure, he should have called her this week, but he worked late every day and then stayed at the shop with his dad and brothers afterward to go over the plans for this week. They made phone calls to volunteers and worked out who had what skills and where they could help out. They contacted the people who were donating items to settle on the delivery day and time, et cetera. By the time he got home, he was exhausted each night. He knew they had a date tonight, so he didn't think any more of it. But she was never far from his mind.

Jeremiah walked over to Ryder and put his arm around Ryder's shoulders. "Hey, your brothers are just teasing; that's all."

"I know, Dad. See, this is what I meant. I don't know what to do. How often I'm supposed to call her. We have a date tonight, and I thought that was good enough. I'm gonna fuck this up."

"No, you aren't. Talk to her. Let her know what you just told me. Honesty is the best policy. Yeah?"

"Yeah," Ryder mumbled as he walked over to a pile of boards that needed to be moved. Physical activity, yep, that's what he needed right now.

Molly and Tammy pulled up the road around seven-fifty to see the street full of parked cars on both sides and a long way from the house. They got out of the car, grabbed Molly's gear and hoisted the bags onto their shoulders as they walked up the street to the house. There was so much activity already. As they approached the yard, they could see the siding had already been removed from the side of Danny's house. There were tables and stations set up everywhere for measuring, sawing, and cutting. They spotted Joci standing by a table that held food and big coffeepots. Molly waved and walked over to her. They hugged, and Molly reminded Joci who Tammy was.

"I have coffee and hot chocolate. Which would you like?"

"Coffee, please," they said in unison.

"I can get it, Joci," Tammy said. As she was pouring their coffees, Molly pulled her camera out.

"We came by yesterday, and I got before pictures. Take a look."

They scrolled through the pictures when Danny walked over.

"Good morning. How are you two this morning?"

"Morning. Glad we came yesterday, with all of this stuff lying around, I wouldn't have been able to get any good before pictures."

Danny nodded and looked around.

"Yeah. I guess it's true what they say, that it needs to get worse before it gets better."

They nodded. Molly looked over and saw Ryder looking their way. She waved at him, but he just scowled and looked away. Molly furrowed her brows. What the heck was *that* for? Molly looked at Tammy, and she shrugged.

"He seemed a little pissed when I told him you were here taking pictures yesterday."

Molly looked at Danny, her brows still furrowed. "He's mad? Because I took pictures?"

Molly looked at Joci. Joci slowly shook her head. "I'm not aware of anyone being upset this morning. But you can bet I'll find out."

Molly shook her head. "Well, I didn't do anything wrong, so whatever. I'm going to snap a few pictures of the progress; then we'll come and help you here for a little while. Is that okay?"

"Sounds good, Molly. Don't worry, hon, I'm sure it's nothing."

Molly shared a look with Tammy, and they walked over to the side of the house where the siding had already been removed. There were probably a hundred volunteers here, and Molly was in her element. She began snapping pictures of the volunteers and the bustle of activity around her.

She took pictures of Joci interviewing Danny on his front porch. Tammy helped with the video camera while Molly continued snapping away.

"Tell me about your time in the service, Danny. Where did you do your basic training?"

"I did my basic at Fort Benning. After basic, I went to Fort Stewart until I was deployed."

"When did you buy this house?"

"I bought it about two years before I went into the Army. I didn't go in straight out of high school; I waited. My dad was sick, and I didn't want to leave. After he passed away, my mom told me she would be fine if I still wanted to go. I did, of course, but was concerned about leaving her. Then, I had this house. Mom and my brother, Paul, took care of it for me while I was gone."

"Tell me about your family. You mentioned that your father passed away, and you have a brother, Paul; any other siblings?"

"No, it was just the two of us. Paul—he's so smart and went to college. He's a veterinarian in town now. He's married to Grace, and they have a baby on the way. Mom still lives in town—close to here, actually."

"When did you know you lost your leg?"

Danny took a deep breath. "I knew almost right away. I couldn't hear my buddies because of the ringing in my ears, and I didn't know if any of them were hurt.

"Finally, one of them knelt down beside me and was talking to me. I couldn't hear what he was saying, but I could tell he was trying to calm me down. Then my other brothers came into my line of vision, and I could see they were surrounding me until they could get me to the helicopter. That helped—knowing they were there. I settled down so I wouldn't freak them out. I passed out in the helicopter; on the way to the base, they told me it was gone."

Tammy was mesmerized by his voice, his eyes, and his story. He didn't feel sorry for himself, and he seemed humbled and overwhelmed by the support he received from Rolling Thunder and the community as a whole. The amount of people who had donated food, materials, tools, and their time to help out was astounding. Danny's eyes welled with tears several times as he spoke. Molly thought he was an incredible human being.

"How did you meet Jeremiah and the Rolling Thunder crew?"

Danny smiled. "I called Jeremiah because I needed to see if my bike could be modified to accommodate my new life. I've always ridden and didn't want to stop. Jeremiah started working with me and, from there, the rest fell into place."

After they had finished the interview, Tammy, Molly, Joci, and Danny walked over to the food table where some local women had gathered with potluck offerings for all the workers. Danny stood between Joci and Molly.

He leaned down and hugged Molly. "Thank you, Molly, for taking the pictures. I'm going to keep an album of them." He leaned close to her ear and said, "I hope everything will be okay with Ryder. I'm sorry I said anything."

Molly looked up at him and smiled. "You're welcome for the pictures; I'll make you a digital photo album. Don't worry about Ryder; I'm sure it's just a misunderstanding. And, if it's okay, I would like to mention that Tammy couldn't stop talking about you last night. She's smitten."

They both chuckled. Tammy looked at Molly with her brows furrowed and Ryder chose that time to turn and see them laughing as Danny's arm rested on Molly's shoulder.

Dammit. She's his. He was going to have to kick Danny's ass if he tried to take Molly from him. Bullshit. Nice guys finish last, and he was sick of being nice. He put his hammer down just as Molly stepped back a few steps to take pictures of the women gathered around the food table. She took a few pictures of Danny and Tammy.

"Can't get enough of taking his picture?" Ryder's voice was tight and low.

Molly glanced at him. "They look good together, don't they?"

Ryder looked over at Danny and Tammy. "Does that piss you off?"

"What? Why would it piss me off? She couldn't stop talking about him last night. What's going on with you today?"

It dawned on Ryder that it was Tammy who was interested in Danny, not Molly. His face flamed a bright red. Fuck. He'd jumped the gun. He sucked at this stuff.

"Fuck. Nevermind." He started to walk away.

Molly grabbed his arm and spun him around to face her. "Hey. Did you think I was interested in Danny? Is that what this is all about? Is that why you scowled at me earlier?"

Ryder looked into Molly's eyes. They stared at each other for a long time. Molly raised her brows.

"Yeah. I thought you were interested in him." His voice was low and soft.

Ryder's heart jumped. He'd never been jealous before, and this was a feeling he didn't like. His stomach was in knots, and his head was all kinds of confused. She smiled at him, a full-on bright smile that made his heart beat so fast he thought it would beat right out of his chest. His gut tightened, his balls drew up, and his cock throbbed when she smiled. She could light up the whole sky. Her dark hair grabbed the shine from the sun and held on to it. Could she be more beautiful?

"Hey. I'm interested in *you*. Even if you didn't call me all week. What are you going to do about it?" Molly asked.

Ryder swallowed and then he couldn't help the smile that spread across his face. She licked her lips and watching that sweet little tongue peek out between her lips almost made him come in his pants. Jesus. He leaned in and kissed her. Softly at first, but Molly immediately lifted her hand and pulled his head down to add more pressure to the kiss. He was lost. He wrapped his arms around her waist and pulled her close. When she was tucked tight to his body, he was stunned at how perfectly she fit against him. He could imagine how she would feel without clothes on and pushed against him. She moaned, and he felt his length grow between them. He wanted her so fucking bad; he had thought of nothing else for the last two weeks.

～

All Molly could think was, *Oh, wow*. He was a fantastic kisser; his lips felt so good against hers—soft, full, and moist. He slipped his tongue between her lips and swirled it around, softly exploring her mouth as she moaned. He suckled on her tongue and her lips, bit her bottom lip and then licked it. She loved that he responded to her so fully. She loved how she felt while wrapped in his arms—safe, protected, and secure—and it felt amazing.

Ryder ended their kiss and laid his forehead against her forehead. "Sorry if I made you feel bad. I shouldn't have assumed."

Molly smiled. "You were jealous."

Ryder's face burned a bright red. He swallowed hard. "Yes."

Molly chuckled. "Why were you jealous?"

"To quote someone I know, I'm not stroking your ego, Molly Bates."

They both laughed. "Come on, let's get you something to eat. You've been working hard this morning."

# 10

## THE DINNER DATE

Molly got out of the shower with pruny hands and feet. She was chilled from being outside all day, so she took an extra long, hot shower, blew her hair dry, dabbed on some makeup, and got dressed. They had worked hard today, so they discussed keeping it casual tonight. She'd been tired leaving Danny's, but the excitement of seeing Ryder kept her going. She hoped he was feeling the same thing.

Dressed in nice jeans, a cream sweater with a dark tan scarf and brown shoe-boots, Molly walked into the kitchen to clean it up a bit. She reflected on the day and on how whenever she looked at Ryder— and it was often--he was watching her as well. Her nether regions had been swollen and moist most of the day. After the way he kissed her, she could think of little more than getting him naked.

The guys worked hard all day as they hoisted the framed-up walls or added a window or door. Molly wanted to capture it all on film so when she was close to Ryder, he would put his arm around her and give her a squeeze or a quick kiss. He always acknowledged her in some way. He wasn't as shy around her as he had been.

It wasn't long before her doorbell rang. She wiped her hands and opened the door. Oh. My. God. Yummy.

"Hi. Come on in."

"You look beautiful, Molly. Wow." Ryder's gaze raked her from head to toe.

Molly blushed at the way he stared at her. He had a way of looking at her as if she were the only woman in the world. God help her, she wanted to be the only woman in his world. She really did.

"Come on in. Do you want a drink first?"

R yder stepped into Molly's living room and took a deep breath. It smelled like her. She smelled spicy in some way, but also like a fresh spring day. It was hard to put into words. It was unique to her and it had teased his senses for the past two weeks. His fingers itched to touch her. He wanted to run his fingers through her hair and pull her close. Today had been fun. When she was close to him, he would pull her in for a kiss or a hug. He loved having her that close and working with others like they had.

"Nah, I'm afraid if I have a drink and sit down, I'll fall asleep on you. Why don't we head out?"

Molly nodded. "I'll just get my jacket."

Ryder watched her walk to the closet. Her ass swayed in the most fantastic way. She filled out a pair of jeans like nobody else. The white sweater she wore wrapped around her breasts and made his hands itch to touch her. He simply thought everything about her was amazing. When she turned and walked toward him, he looked into her eyes. She smiled at him, which caused the usual reaction in his stomach, those butterflies swarmed and his heart beat furiously.

There simply wasn't a part of his body that didn't react to Molly. As soon as she was within reach, he pulled her to him in a hug.

He leaned down and kissed her lips. He meant to just give her a light kiss, but as soon as his lips touched hers, there was no turning back. His arms pulled her body to him while his mouth captured hers. He licked along the seam of her lips and when she opened, his tongue sought the inside of her mouth with a mind of its own. He needed to touch her everywhere. He wanted to taste her and feel her and, my God, he was hungry but not for food, he was ravenous for her.

Her arms wrapped around him and pulled him closer. As their kiss deepened, Ryder's hands slid down her shoulders and the front of her body to touch her breasts. He squeezed her right breast in his hand, cupping the back of her head with his other. When he heard her moan he gently pinched her nipple and he felt her quiver. He kneaded it between his thumb and forefinger, lightly pinching and rubbing to ease the pain of the pinch, first one breast then the other and back again. When he needed more contact, he slid his arms around her and cupped her ass in both hands and pulled her close to him so she could feel his desire pushing against her.

She whimpered and tightened her arms around him and nibbled at his bottom lip. He pushed against her with more pressure and she bit his lip and he felt the air push out of her lungs and into his mouth. His hands shook as the excitement of being with her took over and for the first time in, well, ever, the thought of losing control and being who he always wanted to be hit him with a force that could have knocked him over had she not been holding on so tight. Her hands slid down his chest and abdomen and gripped the bottom of his shirt. She pushed her hands up under his shirt and the feeling of her hands on his bare skin sent a raging inferno through his entire body. His breathing came in jagged spurts and his hands were everywhere.

"Jesus," he hissed out.

Feeling her hands on his bare skin was unbelievable. Ok, fair is fair.
He reached down and pulled Molly's shirt up to expose her tummy
and higher still until her breasts were exposed to him. He reached up
and ran the backs of his fingers along the swell of her breasts and
heard her suck in her breath. He looked down at her while he
continued to rain feather light touches her breasts. Neither said
anything for a few moments until he reached in and pulled a breast
out of her bra. He expertly rolled her nipple between his thumb and
forefinger, forming it into a hard peek. Instinctively, Molly pushed
her pussy into Ryder's hard length and ground back and forth.

His green eyes bore into her blues , he didn't have to say anything.
She pulled her jacket off and let it fall to the floor.

"I'll make us something here later."

He swallowed as he pulled his jacket off in record time and let it fall
on top of hers. Molly grabbed his hand, pulling him toward her
bedroom.

Once inside the bedroom, she turned to him and he pulled her close
once more, walking her backward to the bed. He continued kissing
her while reaching down and undoing the button and zipper on her
jeans. As soon as he had them open, he slid his fingers down the front
of her pants inside her panties and touched her sensitive bud. Molly
gasped as he touched her. His fingers sought her dampness and
found it quickly. He slid his fingers through her damp folds and
found her bundle of nerves as his fingers ran down to her entrance
and back up again, bringing her moisture back to her clit. "Jesus,
Molly, you're so fucking wet. Fuck...what that does to me."

Ryder inhaled deeply pulling her scent deep into his lungs. Her voice
and the sounds she made drove him mad. She responded to him in a
way he had only dreamed of.

Molly pushed her hips up into his fingers. Sensing her closeness, he
drew his hand out of her jeans and pulled her sweater up and over
her uplifted arms. He tossed it to the end of the bed and quickly

reached around finding her bra strap and unhooked it before she took another breath. Her bra came loose and her breasts spilled out into his hands.

"Damn, Molly. You're so fucking beautiful. Jesus." His breath hissed out of his mouth, his jaw tense.

Ryder quickly pulled his shirt off and started undoing his jeans. Molly stopped his hands with hers and smiled as she began lowering the zipper. She looked up into his eyes; the intensity he saw nearly took his breath away. She slowly slid her hands into the waistband and slid them over his tight hips, her hands brushing his heated skin as his jeans fell to the floor. Without a word, her hands cupped his ass and pulled him into her body.

Ryder stood still as he watched Molly divest him of his clothing. Holy crap, he didn't know if he would stop breathing if he moved. His heart beat a rhythm so sharp and strong he thought it would burst out of his chest. He let out a slow, measured breath to calm himself as his hand slid into her hair at the nape of her neck and cupped the back of her head. He leaned in and kissed her soft lips. Her moan shot straight to his cock and robbed him of any patience he was trying to control.

He tugged her jeans enough to allow them to slip over her slim hips and hit the floor. His fingers found the thin strip of lace she called panties and slid inside and around to her beautiful firm ass as he squeezed, eliciting another moan from her. He pulled back just enough to look into her eyes.

His mouth ran dry as her eyes met his and then moved over his body. She traced his dragon tattoo with her fingers, the head was lying over his shoulder the tail wound its way around his arm. She whispered. "It's beautiful." As she admired his dragon, he rolled her nipples between his thumbs and fingers forcing them into tight little peaks. His mouth watered. When she looked up into his eyes, she froze and he heard her breath hitch.

Ryder laid her on the bed, coming down on top of her in one smooth motion. He moved his legs so he was between hers and spread her legs open wide with his knees. He kissed her, deeply, urgently plunging his tongue into her mouth. He completely ravaged her lips, her tongue, and her mouth. Never had he felt so alive—so turned on.

Needing air he left her mouth to trail kisses down her jaw to her neck, where he nipped and bit her lightly, continuing down to her breasts. He sucked first one nipple into his mouth and bit it with his teeth, then the next one. He went back and forth between her breasts a few times then began a slow trail of kisses down her stomach, across her hips, and finally finding her pussy. Her skin was warm under his mouth, soft and supple. His lips were made for her, to touch her skin, and taste her body. He licked her from her opening all the way up to her clit, circling his tongue around and then sliding back down to her opening. She moaned loudly and he heard her soft pants and whimpers. He smiled against her soft folds when she groaned, and he did it all again.

He wanted her groaning. He wanted her panting and quivering and coming in his mouth. Then, he would have her come again while he was inside of her. Maybe a few times before the night was over. He'd been a bastard for the past two weeks. Since the minute he met her, all he could think of was this--tasting her, touching her, being inside of her. Molly groaned again and he slid two fingers inside of her. Her thighs began quaking and her breath escaped her lungs at the same time. He sucked her clit as he flicked it with his tongue. He flattened his tongue out and began a rhythm that sent Molly flying over the edge in no time. When she cried out his name his heart soared and he felt primal and virile and so damn excited.

He lapped at her juices, letting her come down from her high, slowly rolling his tongue over her sensitive tissues. He began kissing his way up her body, paying attention to her flat stomach, her ample breasts, and finally, her mouth. As he kissed her he leaned over and grabbed the condom he had tossed onto the bed earlier. He sat back and opened the wrapper and quickly sheathed himself before settling back over her. He kissed her sweetly and slowly as he pushed himself inside of her. They both groaned at the feel of him pushing into her. He could feel every inch as it was encased in her warmth. He groaned as he slid in and out a few times. Perfect fit.

"Jesus, Molly. You feel so fucking good. Never in my life has anything felt like this."

She mumbled. "Yes. So amazing."

He reached back and pulled one of her legs up and over his arm so he could seat himself fully inside of her. They both moaned as he slid in farther, his rhythm increased as Molly's hips met him with every thrust--both of them thrusting and pushing to make the other reach their pinnacle. Faster and faster they moved until neither could hold back anymore.

"Come on, baby, I need you to come again. You feel so good, Molly."

He thrust into her, harder and faster, knowing he couldn't hold out much longer. She gasped as she came and with a soft moan he pushed himself fully inside of her and froze as he flowed inside of her body. He could feel her walls sucking him off, pulsing and squeezing him. Fucking amazing. He was ruined for any other woman. No one would ever feel like Molly felt.

They lay there for long minutes. Ryder pulled out and rolled off her to discard the condom. He came back to her quickly and pulled her tight to his body. She wrapped her arms around him and sighed in his ear.

"Molly. I don't even know what to say."

Molly sighed. "I know. Me either."

~

L eaning up on her elbow, she looked down at him. She searched his eyes, looking to see if he was happy. What she saw, stole her breath. His face was beautiful, serene and yes, happy. It was a look she always wanted to see.

She lifted her hand and sifted it through Ryder's hair. "Are you hungry? I can go and find something to make for supper."

Ryder sighed contentedly, leaned up and kissed her forehead. "I'm a little hungry, but I promised to take you out. Did you want to get dressed and go somewhere?"

"No. I want to stay here. I have pizza, how about that? We can eat picnic style on the sofa."

"Okay. I'll help you."

They traipsed to the kitchen after dressing and began making their pizza. Molly pulled two beers out of the refrigerator and started Ryder on grating cheese while she added extra pepperoni. She peeked over at him and smiled at the concentration on his face. His forehead pinched together in the middle, his eyes watching the shredded cheese fall into the bowl. She giggled and he looked up. "What?"

She shook her head. "You are certainly concentrating on the cheese, haven't you ever done that before?"

He huffed out a breath. "I'm trying to do a good job for you. Don't make fun of me." He continued looking at his freshly shredded cheese.

Her brows raised into her bangs, she hadn't meant to offend him. Then she saw him smile. Tossing a neatly folded towel at him she giggled. He caught the towel as it plopped on his head and chuckled. He set the chunk of cheese on the cutting board and gently slid the bowl of cheese toward her. His lopsided grin caused the butterflies in her tummy to flutter then he picked up his beer bottle and drank from it. She watched his throat work as he swallowed. She couldn't look away if she wanted to. He simply was the most handsome man she had ever known and, she'd just had sex with him. Score.

He set his bottle on the counter and caught her gaze. One side of his mouth lifted in a grin and her face flushed pink and heated at being caught staring. She quickly busied herself with topping the pizza with the freshly shredded cheese and popped it into the oven.

He cleared his throat. "Did you get good pictures today? It looked like you were taking a ton of them."

"Yeah. I haven't really looked at them yet, but I think I got some pretty good ones. Usually, you only get about one good picture out of twenty or so. Would you want to take a look at them with me?"

"Yeah, I would."

She checked on the pizza, then grabbed her tablet. They walked to the living room and sat together on the sofa as she pulled up the pictures. The before pictures came into view and Ryder smirked as she scrolled through. When the flower pictures appeared, Ryder said, "Danny was worried today when he saw workers getting close to the flowers. I think you made him realize how nice they are."

"They're beautiful flowers. With the sun streaming through the leaves and petals showcasing the vibrant color on the flowers, I just couldn't help myself. We forget about the natural beauty of things sometimes. At that moment, I just couldn't resist taking those pictures." She moved to the next picture and softly smiled. "When I showed them to Danny, he thanked me for showing him the beauty around his house. I think he's still dealing with things from the war and he seems kind of lonely."

Ryder nodded. "I was shocked to hear you were there yesterday. It kind of caught me off guard. He said you were 'hot,' by the way."

She laughed and continued scrolling through pictures. Ryder smiled at pictures of his family and some of the guys. The funny looks on the guys' faces in a couple of the action shots made them chuckle.

"I love these action shots so much; they're real and not posed or phony. All these people were there to help out a veteran today. Joci and I talked about it and I wanted to make sure I captured each volunteer. They should be proud of what they did today too.

"Your mom is going to love these for the video. She's doing a fabulous job with the video and marketing plan for it."

"She is. The video turned out amazing. She showed it to us at the summer party this year and we were blown away. Then she told us it wasn't finished because she wanted to add this last piece to it. We've never had that for the Veteran's Ride before. The end result is going to sell well because, she's right, people love a good cause. They donate to the Veteran's Ride, sometimes just to ride, knowing the money is going to help someone. People will appreciate and remember for a long time where and how the money was spent. And, showing the pictures of the build, with people laughing and looking like they are enjoying the whole thing, will help us find more and more volunteers in years to come."

Molly smiled as he praised his stepmom and at his insight, he wasn't just a pretty face; he understood the benefits behind the event and the importance of marketing future rides like this one. She also liked the look on his face when he spoke about his family. He was so sexy on the outside, and, deep down on the inside, he was a man who loved his family. He was a good person to embrace this cause, not because it made his father's company money, but because it helped somebody. They ate their pizza and drank a couple beers as they settled in and enjoyed their time together.

"So, your dad served in Desert Storm?"

"Yep. My father served with the Marines during Desert Storm with Sarge, Superman, Pitbull, and Radio--you met them at the wedding.

JT and I served in Afghanistan during Operation Enduring Freedom."

"That must have been hard. Did you know Danny from there?"

"No. I didn't know about him until dad started working with him to build his bike. With his leg gone, we needed to modify the controls. Dad instantly liked Danny and through conversation, he found out that he struggled a bit with the steps in his home. That's how Dad decided Danny would be this year's recipient."

"Well, I would like to say thank you for your service and I think it's great that your dad does this event every year."

Ryder turned toward her and let out a long breath. "You know, I was in Afghanistan for over a year." He raised his brows and turned his perfect lips into a pout.

She studied him and wrinkled up her face. He smirked at her and she got the hint of how to properly thank him for his service. She smiled and crawled over his lap straddling his legs. She touched each side of his face with her hands and ran her thumbs across his cheeks. Looking deep into his eyes, she leaned down and kissed him, her lips lightly brushed across his, nipping and tasting. She slipped her tongue into his mouth at the same time her hands slid behind his neck and up the back of his head.

Ryder's hands grabbed Molly's ass and pulled her into his erection firmly. With gentle pressure, he pushed and pulled her so she was grinding against him. He didn't have to push and pull much; she caught on and began rubbing against him on her own. He groaned into her mouth when her sweet hips moved on their own. She continued her invasion of his mouth, holding his head in place while her hips continued their assault on his cock.

Molly was losing herself in this man. She liked talking to him. He was smart, caring, and deeply committed to his family and their cause. He was hot beyond words and he felt so damn good when he kissed her *and* when he was inside of her. She wanted him there again and quickly.

She whispered. "Ryder, I'm going to come very soon. That doesn't seem like a proper thank you for your service, so we need to get naked, so I can thank you properly."

"No argument here, babe."

She stood and removed her clothing. Ryder had his shirt off and his pants undone before she finished undressing. He sat back on the sofa and she quickly straddled him again. He grabbed her ass with both of his hands and pulled her forward to rub against his cock.

"Oh," was all Molly could say.

"**Y**eah." He didn't want to talk right now; he wanted to fuck fast and hard. That's what she did to him.

He lifted her enough to position his cock just beneath her. He reached up with this fingers to feel her wetness and sucked in a breath when she moaned. He quickly pulled a condom on and as soon as the head of his cock touched her she plunged down impaling herself on him. Both of them groaned as he stretched her wide and filled her.

"Jesus, that feels fucking amazing." He huffed out. He realized that less than an hour ago he had spilled himself inside of her, yet it felt like he hadn't fucked her at all. This time was as amazing as the first.

She had beautiful breasts. They were full and heavy, perfectly shaped, round mounds with delicious pink nipples. Right now, her nipples were tight and peaked and he wanted them in his mouth. They looked like the most delicious candy. He grabbed them in his hands and massaged them as she rode him. He pulled her tight little nipples into his mouth and sucked on them. He heard a harsh breath escape her lips as he sucked her in and looked up at her.

His nostrils flared and his mouth roved between her breasts. She mewled and it nearly took his breath away. He reached around and squeezed her ass and pulled her forward setting a new pace that was fevered and fast. Raising his hips as he pulled her forward and pushed down pushing him deeper into her. She cried out and tightened her hands in his hair.

"You are seriously the most beautiful woman I've ever seen." He managed to huff out. "Let go, Molly."

She groaned as he hit her deep inside and she burst with an orgasm that rocked him like never before. The look on her face was ecstasy, the shudders that wracked her body excited him but the way she cried out his name. Well, that was mind-blowing. He wrapped his arms around her while she came undone on top of him. Overwhelmed with these unfamiliar feelings his heart raced. He nibbled at her neck and ears while she continued to explode around him. His arms tightened around her as he whispered in her ear how good she felt and how beautiful and special she was and how she had ruined him for any other woman. She whimpered and opened her eyes. Staring into his, we watched emotions float through them like clouds in the wind.

He began moving inside of her. He held her hips in place as he pushed up into her. "My turn." He huffed out. In and out, slowly, using all of his control. He wanted to bring her up again and tumble with her when she came. He watched her face as he slid in and out, her beautiful eyes never left his. Her full lips were slightly opened and that maddening little tongue darted out to wet her lips catching his attention.

He wrapped his arms around her waist and flipped her over on her back, allowing him to change the pace. He reached down and grabbed her leg and pulled it up and over the back of the sofa so he could push into her further. Hearing her groan as he slid all the way inside of her made him feel powerful. So fucking good. Nothing in the world could ever feel like this.

Increasing the pace, his body heat rose, a fine sheen of sweat covered his chest and back. "I'm going to take you fast and hard now, Molly. Ready?"

She rasped out. "God, yes...please...fast and hard."

He obliged, pounding into her as hard and as fast as he could. The only sound in the room was their sweaty flesh slapping against each other and Molly's moans. Her hands grabbed his ass and pulled him in as he was pushing, urging him in hard and fast.

He ground out. "Now...Molly. Now."

One more thrust and he felt her stiffen and groan as he held himself inside of her and released his hot seed. He pulsed as his breathing started to return. Fucking intense. He lost his vision for a moment, and everything went black around him.

He collapsed on her for just a few moments before raising up on his arms. He kissed her forehead, each eye lid, her nose, her cheeks and softly and tenderly, her lips. He pulled out to remove the condom, wrapped it in his discarded napkin and turned to pull her into his arms. She turned to her side and willingly snuggled into his chest and wrapped her arm around him. They rested in silence for a few minutes before Molly took a deep breath and said. "Ryder? Never in my life...I mean...I never had...um...wow! I can't say anything except, wow."

He chuckled. "I know. I don't have words either. My mind is trying to process that, but, it can't."

They lay there for a while and Ryder felt himself starting to drift off to sleep. He felt right here--like he belonged here and she made him feel so good. He moved to sit up while Molly turned to sit along side him.

She stifled a yawn. "Sorry, I think I was starting to doze off."

"Me too. It's been a long day and we have to do it again tomorrow." He hesitated and rubbed the back of his neck. "I don't want to leave, Molly."

Her voice was breathy. "Yes. Stay here and hold me."

They stood and he pulled his jeans on. Molly whispered, "I'll go grab my robe.

He grabbed her by the arm and pulled her to him, kissed the top of her head and wrapped his arms around her. After a few moments, he felt her shiver and pulled back to see goose bumps on her skin. "Here, wear this." He said as he pulled his t-shirt over her head.

She looked down at his shirt covering her to mid-thigh and smiled up at him. "Sexy...right?"

"Damn sexy."

They cleaned up their leftover supper and put the dishes in the dishwasher. She turned from the sink, looked up into his eyes and smiled. As she wrapped her arms around him and moved close, he immediately pulled her into a hug and it felt so perfect, so right.

She felt his cock twitch as her breasts rubbed across his chest. Her nipples were hard and erect, and his scent called to her. His beautiful body—muscles sculpted from working out--fit so perfectly against hers. And that tattoo--it made her wet just thinking about it. Without thinking, she moved back and forth, rubbing her nipples against his belly and chest. She heard him suck in a breath and looked up. Her heart pounded in her chest. His green eyes sparkled with such intensity that her breath caught in her throat.

"Do you realize how sexy you are, Molly? You are without a doubt the sexiest woman I've ever met."

She watched his eyes, his face. He looked at her like he meant every word. She could see the sincerity in his eyes.

He picked her up and carried her to the bedroom. Butterflies flew untethered in her tummy. She'd never been carried off to bed before, it was trilling. He lay her on the bed gently and climbed in next to her, pulling the blankets around them, he wrapped his arms around her. She lay with her head on his arm and her arms wrapped securely around him, enjoying the comfort and loving feelings playing a song in her heart.

# 11

## NOVEMBER

"Okay, now Gunnar—turn a little to the right. Perfect. Smile, everyone. Keep smiling."

Molly clicked away with her camera. Of course, she had the sexiest subjects on the planet. Jeremiah and Joci liked her idea of using the boys in the marketing for Rolling Thunder, so they set up a photo shoot at the shop. They wore Rolling Thunder shirts Joci had designed and had made for the employees and others that were for sale. There were button-up, short sleeve shirts, short sleeve t-shirts, and long sleeve t-shirts all in a myriad of colors. The employees could wear any style they chose as long as it had the Rolling Thunder logo on it. And all of the different styles and colors gave Molly plenty of opportunity to play around with the boys. She had to admit, they took this modeling seriously because it was for Rolling Thunder, but she enjoyed making them uncomfortable. At one point, she had Gunnar face JT and put his nose super close to JT's nose. She said, "Closer. Closer. Closer." Until Gunnar snapped. "This is bullshit. We're not taking pictures like that." She burst out laughing and had to endure a few glares for a while afterward. After all, she had told Gunnar, 'Paybacks are a bitch.'

Currently, Ryder was wearing a gray, button-up shirt. Gunnar had on a light tan button-up and JT was wearing an orange button-up. Molly posed them in front of the Rolling Thunder logo on the shop wall. She had shot several poses of them in various shirts and positions. JT wasn't initially excited about being 'pimped out' for the shop, but he got into it rather quickly. He was the one of all of them who enjoyed the attention. Women always came into Rolling Thunder to 'check him out.' They would pretend to look at clothes, but they were looking around hoping to be the one to catch his eye. The giggles in the store were a commonplace occurrence. Molly was thankful Ryder worked in the back; she'd have a hard time dealing with the constant female attention.

She and Ryder had been dating for about five weeks now, and things seemed to be going along well. Her business was thriving, especially with all the Rolling Thunder work coming her way. Joci's video had been on sale for just two weeks, and they had already sold fifteen hundred copies. With a special thank you to Molly for the build photos on the end credits, she'd been getting tons of phone calls for work. She was grateful to Joci and thanked her every chance she got.

"How're they coming?" Joci walked into the room and smiled at her boys. She was four months pregnant now and had a cute little baby bump.

"Great!" Molly winked. "Of course, the subject matter helps."

"Okay guys, I think I have enough for today. Thank you."

Ryder jumped down off the platform and walked straight to Molly. He kissed her soundly, making her blush, knowing his mom was standing right there. A blush crawled up her neck and stained her cheeks, but she loved it.

Joci chuckled and walked back to the stairs leading up to the offices she shared with Jeremiah. "Don't forget dinner on Sunday. It's a special one this week."

"I won't." Molly chuckled.

"So how did they turn out, babe?"

"Great. You guys are amazing models. These ads are going to be fabulous. Just don't forget about me when you're famous."

Molly was half joking. He could easily be famous; in fact, all of them could. If that happened, she hoped he would never forget her. She knew she would never forget him.

"Don't be like that, Molly. I'll never forget you as long as I live."

Relief washed through her at hearing him say it. She wondered if he loved her. She both hoped he did and didn't. She hadn't said anything to him about her past, and she was so afraid to take that next step. No matter how many times her friends told her she was nothing like her mom, she just couldn't escape the doubts.

"So, about this special dinner on Sunday. Are we supposed to get Gunnar a gift or something?"

"Beats me. I've never been to an adoption party. I suppose if he were a baby, you would give a gift, but he's grown, for God's sake. JT and I talked about it, and we thought since he's changing his last name, we would get him something monogrammed with *Gunnar Sheppard* on it. What do you think? I've meant to talk to you about it. We could get him something together—from the three of us."

"That sounds like a great idea. What did you have in mind?"

"Well, Dad already has the signs for the shop in his office. We have signs above our workstations with our names on them, so that's done. They also ordered his business cards with his new name on them. We use those for appointments when people come in and make them in person. So, we were kind of at a loss. What do you think?"

"Hmm. What about a nice wooden chest or jewelry valet with his name on it? Or something for his bike? Or a shirt or something with just his initials."

Ryder pulled his wallet out and pulled out his credit card. "Will you go and pick something out for us three? Spend a fair amount on it. A guy only changes his name once in his life, you know."

They both laughed; this was something new altogether. Jeremiah had asked Gunnar if he would want to be adopted and have the Sheppard last name. Since Joci was pregnant and the baby would obviously be a Sheppard, Gunnar would be the only one in the family who wasn't, so Jeremiah wanted him to feel like he was one of them. Jeremiah loved him just as much as his own sons and Gunnar loved Jeremiah, so he agreed right away. Gunnar had only met his biological father, Keith, once, and that had been while his mom was in the hospital, so there was no love lost there. Just recently, Keith had passed away from lung cancer, so the time couldn't be more perfect.

"Sure. I'll pick something up and show you tonight. Are you coming home for supper?"

Ryder smiled at her and raised his brows. She cocked her head and pursed her lips. "What?"

"You said 'coming home for supper.' That sounded good. Home with you sounds *damn* good."

Her mouth dropped open as she stared into his eyes. A bright smile split her lips as she nodded. "That does sound good."

"Yes. I'll be *home* for supper."

Molly turned to walk out, and Ryder smacked her on the ass. She smirked as she walked away, not looking back. It did feel good using the word home with Ryder. He had been staying there a lot. He had his toothbrush, toiletries, extra clothes, and shoes there. She had some things at his place, but they didn't go there much. She felt weird with JT and Gunnar there, so they usually stayed at her place.

Molly shopped for Gunnar's gift before going home to make supper. As she was putting a casserole in the oven, her phone rang.

"Memories by Molly... Yes, this is she... Oh, I'm so sorry to hear that. Is there anything I can do? ...I'm so sorry. My condolences ...Yes, that's true ...Oh, thank you; yes, I'm very interested...Yes, tomorrow will be fine. I'll see you then."

Molly turned around, and Ryder was standing in the kitchen listening to her.

"Good news?"

"Yes...well, yes and no. My landlord, Ellison Jepson, passed away yesterday. That was his son, Jeffrey, on the phone. He wants to talk with me about buying this house. I had a verbal agreement with Mr. Jepson, but he apparently wrote it down. So, Jeffrey is coming here tomorrow to talk with me about purchasing the house."

"That's awesome, Molly." He walked forward and wrapped her in his arms.

"Kind of scary. I've treated this place like my own, knowing that Mr. Jepson and I had an agreement. But now, it's kind of overwhelming thinking that this is it. What if the terms he offers aren't acceptable? What if I can't afford what he will ask for it?"

"First of all, don't worry about any of that until you speak with him. If he needs to get rid of Mr. Jepson's assets to settle the estate, he may just offer you a great price to get all of this settled. As far as not being able to afford it—if you need help, I'll help you, Molly. I have some money saved, and I make enough money at the shop. I'll help you in any way I can."

~

He'd had been thinking about this for a while now—living with Molly. He wanted to live with her anywhere she wanted to live.

"After you had asked me if I was coming home for supper, I realized that wherever you are is home for me; maybe we could buy this house together."

Molly's eyes rounded and she was looking in his direction, but it didn't seem as though she was seeing him. She tightened her fist in the bottom of her blouse and tugged on it. When she didn't respond, his brows drew together.

"Hey. Where are you?"

She blinked and softly said, "Sorry. I was just thinking."

"Molly? Hey, talk to me."

Ryder stepped forward and placed his hands on her upper arms. He leaned in and looked into her eyes for answers, a response, anything. Her eyes finally registered his nearness, and she cleared her throat.

"Ryder. Umm, I don't know what to say."

She wiped her eyes with her fingers, and his heart felt like it was going to beat right out of his body. He knew he hadn't misjudged them. He thought she was as much into him as he was into her. They were great together, and he never wanted to be with anyone else.

Softly he said, "Molly, I love you. I think I've loved you since the first day we met. I didn't know it then—what it was—but there was something pulling me to you. The first time we made love, I knew it without a doubt; I knew I was in love with you. That was the first time I'd ever *made love*. Before, it was just...fucking, the need for release. Moving in together is the natural next step." He took a breath and stepped back. He rubbed his jaw and slid his hand around to the back of his neck. "If you don't want to buy the house with me, I get it. I just wanted you to know that I was here for you if you needed me. Don't get me wrong; I would love to buy this house with you, but this was something you had going on before I ever came on the scene. I'm not trying to steal it from you."

Molly's head snapped up. "You love me? Really?"

Ryder snorted. "Good God, can't you tell? My brothers have been giving me shit for weeks now. I am so head-over-heels in love with you, I can't believe it."

~

M olly giggled. Yes, giggled. He loved her! Relief is what she felt. Those three unspoken words did stupid things to her head. She imagined the worst all the time, when she should have just been honest with him a while ago and told him she loved him.

"Ryder, I love you, too. I have for a while now. I was just afraid to say it."

He grabbed her and pulled her in for a hug. He hung on to her for several moments, and she enjoyed the feel of him against her, loving the words that he had just spoken.

"God, I love you, Molly."

She chuckled. "I love you too, Ryder."

It just felt good to say it. It felt good to hear it.

"Hey, no pressure. It's all good. Let's take it one step at a time," he mumbled into her hair.

"I just don't want to be like my mom. I'm scared that I'll be her; I don't know what to do."

Tears fell from her eyes, and Ryder continued to hold her close, crooning sweet words into her ear as he comforted her. He steered her to the sofa and sat with her while she cried herself out. When it felt like she could speak again, he got her a cloth from the bathroom and wet it with warm water. He brought it to her so she could wipe her face and hands, but sat quietly while she pulled herself together, letting her collect her thoughts.

"You've said that before—you don't want to be like your mom—but I don't know what that means. Last month when you went to the nursing home, you didn't ask me to go with you. It bothered me, but I tried to move past it. I want to understand."

Molly nodded. She smiled weakly and sat back on the sofa.

"I do owe you an explanation. I'm sorry I broke down. I've been so worried for so long." She sighed and glanced over at him. "I knew it hurt your feelings last month when I went to see my mom. I'm sorry about that, Ryder. It was never my intention to hurt you—never."

She took a deep breath. This conversation was long overdue. "When I was eleven, my mom and stepdad divorced. After that, my mom drank...a lot. She went from man to man after that." Her hands gently moved in front of her as she spoke. "They would move into our house until they couldn't stand my mother and her drinking, then the next man would move in. My mom just couldn't be without a man. She was weak; she drank, and she always needed someone to make her feel valued."

She watched his jaw clench and then he took a deep breath and let it out slowly. When he spoke, it was soft and gentle. "You're not her, Molly. Look at you; you have your own business, and you're independent. Living with me doesn't change that." He glanced around the room, seeming to take it all in. "It just makes both of our lives richer. You don't identify yourself by me. You identify yourself by you. You know that, right?"

"I do...I guess. She did some horrible things to people when she was younger; I suppose out of desperation. I don't want to be that person."

"Well, I know without a doubt you're not that person. Please don't let something your mom did years ago keep us from moving forward in our relationship. That's a cruel, cruel punishment for no reason at all." He leaned forward and gently pressed his lips to hers.

She nodded and wiped under her eyes with the cloth. The oven timer signaled time to eat. Molly softly smiled and stood to move into the kitchen. She pulled the casserole from the oven while Ryder set the table. They ate in relative silence, each lost in their own thoughts.

After they had eaten, Ryder sat back in his chair and rubbed his full belly. "You're a great cook, babe. That was delicious."

She smiled her brightest smile and whispered, "Thank you."

They spent the evening sitting on the sofa with the TV on and neither of them paying attention to what was blasting away on the tube. He didn't know what else he could say to make her understand that she wasn't like her mom. He thought maybe he could talk to his mom about it and see what she thought. Maybe that's what he would do. Surely, she could talk some sense into Molly. He had a niggling feeling that wasn't all to her story, but it seemed so hard for her to tell him things about her past. So he decided to be patient with her since there wasn't anything that would make him think less of her. Eventually, she would know that.

"Have you ever lived with anyone else?" He held his breath, waiting for Molly to respond. Maybe that's what was bugging her.

She pinched her eyebrows together and slowly turned her head. The look on her face was one of confusion.

"No. I never have."

His breath escaped his lungs in a whoosh. Then he chuckled and shook his head.

"Stupid to ask. I just wondered."

He watched her smile slowly spread across her face. "You were worried. Not about me being like my mom, but you want to be the first to live with me, don't you?"

A blush tinted his cheeks and the tips of his ears. He nodded and looked down at his hands.

"Would you like to move in with me?" she asked softly as she leaned toward him.

She stared at him, a beautiful smile on her face. His eyes grew round, and a grin spread across his entire face. He hesitated, swallowed, and then spoke.

"Are you sure?"

"Yes, I am. You're right! I can't let my mom's past behavior keep me from having a good life of my own. That's not fair to either one of us and to be honest, if she knew that's what I was doing, she would hate it. She wasn't a great mom, but I do believe she loved me."

He smirked and rubbed the back of his neck. "Well, I don't know now... I'll have to think about it," he chuckled.

Her brows furrowed. She giggled and threw a pillow at him. Laughing, he caught it and tossed it to the floor before wrapping her up in his arms.

## 12

---

# JEFFREY

After making love through the night, Molly woke early, excitement and nerves running through her over the purchase of the house and Ryder moving in. She scooted from the bed and showered while he slept. She made a pot of coffee and took a cup to the bedroom, sat on the bed next to him, set his cup on the nightstand, and ran her hand through his hair.

She softly crooned. "Hey sleepyhead, wake up."

He groaned and pulled her close to him. He quickly opened his eyes and looked at her clothing.

"Why are you up and dressed already? I thought we could have a little more fun."

Molly laughed. "Good lord, you're a horny one. Didn't you get enough of me last night?"

"I'll never get enough of you. If I'm horny, it's entirely your fault. You smell good; you look good, and you feel good. I'm completely unable to keep my hands off of you."

She stiffened, closed her eyes, took a deep breath and let it out slowly. She sat back and collected herself. She grinned slightly. "Good to know. Jeffrey Jepson is coming over this morning to discuss my purchase of the house. I was too nervous and excited to sleep anymore."

He sat up and scraped his hands through his hair and down his face. He looked at her closely, his eyes roving over her face and her posture. Uncomfortable with his perusal, she handed him his cup of coffee, and he smiled at her.

"Thanks, babe. You're incredible," he complimented quietly.

He kissed her first, taking her hand and pulling her in, then took a drink of his coffee.

"Mmm. I needed that. Do you need me here with you?"

"If you want to be here, I certainly don't mind. After all, you're living here—or will be. But I know you have work, so I don't expect you to take off for this."

"I'm happy to be here, but only if you're comfortable with it; I don't want to butt in. I know you want to do this yourself."

"Thanks. I appreciate you letting a girl take care of this on her own," she quipped.

"I've never said you aren't capable of this because you're a girl. Which, by the way, is one of the things I love most about you." He chuckled. "I just want you to feel safe and comfortable with all the decisions, and there's nothing wrong with having a second set of ears and eyes when talking about a purchase like this. That's all."

That was true. Molly hadn't thought of that.

"Well, if you don't mind coming back to the house around nine-thirty, I would love to have you here."

Ryder grinned. "Deal. I'll be here at nine-thirty."

She strolled out to the kitchen and pulled eggs and bacon from the refrigerator for breakfast. If she stayed in the bedroom, he'd be late for work, and she wouldn't be ready for her meeting with Jeffrey.

Ryder left a few minutes before eight to head for the shop with the promise to be home at nine-thirty. She cleaned up the breakfast dishes and straightened up the living room, made the bed and picked up dirty clothes. She wanted the house to look nice and to make a good impression on Jeffrey. She wanted this to work out for her and Ryder.

Ryder—forever in her thoughts now—was simply the kind of man she'd often dreamed of. He didn't push her; he just wanted to be part of her life. She had kept him at arm's length for a while now for the pure reason that she didn't want him to wake up one morning and decide she wasn't worth it. So, tonight she would tell him she would be happy if he wanted to buy the house with her. After all, if they did it right and had a contract drawn up, they could do this together. They loved each other. She enjoyed his company, and she liked talking to him. Their evenings together were great; actually, everything they did together was enjoyable. They spent time sharing their days with each other. He shared his family with her without reservation. It was what she'd always hoped for. And she needed to introduce him to her mother, to share with him as much as he shared with her.

Her phone began playing the song, "Memories," her business ring. "Memories by Molly."

"Hello. Molly. Bates." The gravelly voice from her nightmares grated over the phone.

Molly sucked in a breath. Her knees weakened as she sank into a chair in the kitchen.

"How...How did you get my number?"

"Well, you little bitch, you've plastered your name all over the Rolling Thunder DVDs. Your picture, too. It wasn't all that hard to find you."

She swallowed and tried to focus on a spot on the wall. When the spot began to swirl, she closed her eyes and took a deep breath to calm her nerves.

Taking a breath so her voice didn't shake, she commented. "You're not supposed to contact me."

"Says who? Nobody's gonna stop me from contacting you. I told you years ago, you owe me, and you will pay me back. We both know what that means."

Molly hit the *End Call* button on her phone with shaking fingers. She should have known it was all too good to be true. Her breakfast threatened to make a quick exit, and she ran to the bathroom just in time to empty her stomach. She leaned against the edge of the bathroom counter, subconsciously wiping her mouth with a wet cloth when her thoughts were interrupted by a knock on the door. Walking down the hall on shaky legs, she checked the time on her phone—it was only nine-ten. She opened the door to a short, balding, rotund man in his early forties. He wore glasses, and his hair was too long for the small amount he had on his head. The odor something akin to an unbathed body and greasy hair assaulted her nose at the same time he moved his lips to form a half smile.

Molly raised her brows and stood taller. "May I help you?"

"Are you Molly? I'm Jeffrey Jepson." He moved from one foot to the other and his hands were balled at his sides.

She stood back while holding the inside door open. "Yes. Oh, please come in. I wasn't expecting you until nine-thirty."

He hesitated briefly then stepped into the living room. "Yes, sorry about that. I finished my meetings early and wanted to get this one out of the way before I have to go and see the probate attorney. I hope you don't mind."

"Of course not." Molly led him into the kitchen and pointed to the kitchen table.

"Please take a seat. Can I get you a cup of coffee?"

"Yes, black, please."

She watched from the corner of her eye as he sat at the table. She poured him a cup and another one for herself. She didn't know if she should call Ryder or just start without him. Jeffrey seemed to be in a hurry, and she didn't want to keep him. She sat across from him at the table and sipped her coffee.

"How long have you lived here?" He sipped from his cup.

"I've been here five years now. I've done a lot of work, fixing it up hoping that it would be mine one day. I've painted, had the roof replaced as well as all the inside doors." She glanced around the kitchen with pride. "I've replaced the kitchen flooring and was thinking about replacing the bathroom tile this winter. I'm very sorry for your loss, by the way. I really liked Mr. Jepson."

"Thanks. Yes, it looks very nice. You've done a great job." Jeffrey looked around the room, his fingers tapping his coffee cup.

Molly felt tingles run up her spine. She sat straighter but looked him in the eye. It was apparent that he was socially awkward, but it was something a bit more...creepy.

He fumbled in his shirt pocket. "I found this in my dad's safe as I was going through his things. He had just a couple of rentals. As I was digging around trying to locate his assets, I came across this." His voice shook, and it took him a bit to unfold the worn sheet of paper. Once he was able to open it, he handed it to her with shaking fingers.

*Upon my death, if I haven't previously sold the house on Ninth Street to Molly Bates, I would like for it to be sold to her for one hundred-fifteen thousand dollars. We have a verbal agreement, and I would like that agreement honored. Ellison Jepson*

Molly stared at the worn piece of paper; the end ripped at the corner. She held it firmly between her fingers and thumbs, afraid to let it go. The house appraised at so much more than that last year.

Her voice shook as she softly said. "This is very generous. Are you holding to this agreement?"

He nodded but didn't say anything. The warning bells began going off in her head. The way he stared at her was making her jittery. She was very aware that they were alone in the house, and Ryder wasn't due for another few minutes or so, and that was provided he could get away on time. Her heart hammered away in her chest, and her skin grew moist and pink.

"O-okay. Y-yes, I would be happy to buy the house for this price." She let out a breath as her stomach churned.

Jeffrey stood up abruptly. "I would like a tour to see what you've done here."

She felt increasingly uneasy about being alone in the house with him; her mind raced for a stall tactic. She didn't want to be alone with him in the bedroom or back of the house. The price had been established, but she didn't know how to turn him down without offending him or making him change his mind.

She nodded and slowly stood. Jeffrey followed, and she thought the best place to start would be outside. She turned and opened the sliding doors to the patio and held her arm out motioning him outside.

She started by showing him the landscaping she'd done.

"I planted all of the flowers, added the chips and edging and the decorations."

When he made no response, she pointed to the roof. "I had the roof replaced two years ago."

She showed him the section of the fence she had repaired. Now that she had shown him everything she could show him outside, she had no choice but to go inside.

*Please come home soon, Ryder.*

Jeffrey was eerily silent and continued to stare at her. Growing more and more uneasy, she walked into the living room. He walked close to her and touched her shoulder. He reached up and touched her hair, and she jumped. Looking for an excuse to distance herself, she said. "I need another cup of coffee, would you like one?"

"No." His voice had become flat and hard.

She quickly marched into the kitchen and busied herself with her cup. Taking a deep breath, the stench of his unclean body hit her nostrils. She slowly turned to find him standing close behind her— too close—effectively trapping her in the corner of the kitchen. She stepped forward and to the side to walk around him, and he stepped in front of her. Her heart raced, and her breathing became choppy. Her hands began to shake, and all she could think was, *Where is Ryder?*

"What's going on?" Ryder's voice carried the tone of menace, and she visibly shook as a chill ran down her spine.

*Oh, thank God.*

"Hi, babe. Come on in and meet Jeffrey Jepson." She tried to hide the quiver in her voice.

Ryder looked into Molly's eyes then his gaze slid over to Jeffrey Jepson. He strode over and held out his hand to Jeffrey while at the same time, stepping in front of her, hiding her from Jeffrey.

"Ryder Sheppard. Nice to meet you."

"A-a-are you h-her h-husband?" Jeffrey stuttered out.

"Not yet. But soon."

Ryder looked back at Molly and winked. She relaxed and smiled.

"Did I miss anything? I thought the meeting was for nine-thirty."

"Y-yes, I was a little early. I had other meetings this morning and later today, s-so I thought I would come b-by early."

"Oh, well I'm sorry I missed it." She watched his jaw clench.

Ryder reached back and pulled Molly forward, wrapped his arm around her and kissed the top of her head. Jeffrey stepped back and brusquely walked toward the front door, Ryder and Molly on his heels.

"Yes. W-well I'm leaving n-now. I h-have other things to do. I'll leave you t-to work out the details with your bank." He didn't make eye contact as his words stammered from his mouth. He scuttled down the two steps to the sidewalk and scurried away.

As soon as the door closed, Ryder reached forward and locked it. She shook as the chills ran through her body. She reached out and hugged Ryder tight. He tightened his hold on her and softly rubbed her back.

Taking a deep breath, he asked, "Are you okay?"

She nodded, but she couldn't get words out just yet. When she had settled down, she told him, "I was so scared. He gave me the creeps. He wanted a tour of the house, and I didn't want to be alone with him in the bedroom or any small room. I took him out to the backyard first and tried stalling as long as I could." She stepped back and ran her fingers down her face. "We came back in, and I showed him the living room, and he touched my hair. I was scared and went into the kitchen pretending to need more coffee. That's when he came up behind me. Thank God you walked in when you did."

Ryder wrapped his arms tighter around her. "I'll never let anything happen to you, Molly. I'm so sorry I wasn't here."

He calmly rubbed her back as he held her tight to his body, his deep breathing and the rigidity of his posture told her he was fighting to keep his emotions under control. To know he was this affected by her incident made her heart swell.

After calming, she stepped back and showed Ryder the piece of paper Jeffrey had given her. Her fingers shook slightly, but she unfolded it and turned it toward him.

"Look at the price, Ryder. That's a bargain."

He gently took the paper and read Mr. Jepson's note. A grin tilted his lips.

"That's fantastic. And here you were worried for nothing." He touched his lips to hers.

She rested her hands on his hips and looked into the beautiful green eyes she'd so recently fallen in love with. "Do you still want to buy it with me?"

Ryder's brows shot up. "Really? You mean it?"

She nodded. "I was thinking about our conversation last night, and you're right, I can't keep worrying about what my mom did in the past. I love you, Ryder, and I want to move forward with you. We could have a contract written up to protect each of us, in case it doesn't work out, or whatever you want. Just let me know."

He raised his arm in the air and whooped. He picked Molly up and swung her around, both of them laughing when he set her on her feet.

"We should go and talk to my mom and dad. They can give us advice and the name of a good attorney."

～

He didn't need a contract, but if Molly wanted one, he'd be fine. "We'll need a contract written up for the house purchase, and we should make copies of that note Mr. Jepson wrote—in case Jeffrey changes his mind." He glanced out the window.

"In the meantime, if he comes back here, don't let him in this house if I'm not here with you. Hopefully, that was a one-time incident; but just in case, I don't want you alone with that asshole."

"Yes, sir." Molly saluted.

He smiled as he watched the color come back into her face. Seeing that disgusting bastard in the kitchen with her nearly set him on a path Jepson would be sorry he turned down.

# 13

## GUNNAR AND MOLLY

"Congratulations, Gunnar. Do you feel different?" Molly smiled as she watched Gunnar shrug. It was a stupid question, but honestly, what did you say to a twenty-five-year-old man who had just been adopted? It wasn't something Molly had experienced before.

"Yeah, I feel different. I feel great. I finally have a last name I can be proud of."

Gunnar grinned from ear to ear. Jeremiah walked over and put his arm around Gunnar's shoulders, and Molly couldn't help but snap a few pictures with her phone. It wasn't an official photo gig, and Joci told her not to worry about it. Today was a family day and an important one at that.

She and Ryder still hadn't told Gunnar and JT that Ryder was moving in and buying the house with her—they hadn't told anyone. They decided to wait until after tonight. All he needed to move was his clothes, his bike, and his truck. Some of the workout equipment was his, but he was going to leave that there for his brothers. He said he could work out there or buy more for his and Molly's place. A little shiver ran through her at the thought of them buying a house together.

Joci started toward the living room. "Let's go into the living room and open your gifts."

I t was now mid-November, and Thanksgiving was just around the corner. Ryder was happy—incredibly happy. Gunnar officially became his brother today. He'd felt like a brother for a long time now, but today, it was official. Soon, he'd be moving in with the woman he loved with his whole heart. He was so excited about it, but they'd decided to wait until after they had eaten and Gunnar opened his gifts before telling the family. After all, it was Gunnar's day today, not theirs.

Gunnar sat in an armchair to open his gifts. The rest of the family sat in the various chairs or on the sofa as they watched. He ripped into the gift Molly had purchased from her, JT, and himself.

"Sweet. This is awesome. Thanks, you guys...and girl." Gunnar winked at Molly. "You'll have to tell me why you bought me a box with my name on it."

Molly laughed, and Ryder couldn't look away from her beautiful face. Her soft lips curved into the most beautiful smile he'd ever seen. Her blue eyes twinkled when she was happy. She explained. "It's a jewelry-slash-wallet valet. You know, so you can keep your dresser clean and have one place to put your important items before you go to bed each night."

Gunnar pulled two dress shirts with his initials monogrammed on the cuff, and ties to match with Sheppard monogrammed on them from the box. His smile rivaled Molly's but not by much. Gunnar jumped up and kissed Molly on the top of the head and punched JT and Ryder on the shoulders. Ryder guessed that was a brother hug of sorts.

He opened the remainder of the gifts from his family and thanked everyone.

"I have one more special gift for you, Gunnar," Molly said, holding up a small green box with a gold tie wrapped around it.

Gunnar gingerly took the box from Molly and looked at it with his brows furrowed. "You've already given me so much. What's this?"

"This is something very special to me. When I was little, my mom found this amazing little chocolate shop, Seroogies. It was our treat for special occasions. These were the treats she would buy me every year for my birthday and Christmas and anytime I hit some sort of milestone in my life. Open it." Molly clapped her hands together.

Gunnar smirked and began opening the box. As he opened the lid, the most delicious aroma wafted up to his nostrils. Chocolate. Glorious chocolate. There, nestled in a gold foil tray, were 12 round morsels wrapped in gold. He picked one out of the box and unwrapped the foil wrapping and smiled. As he bit down, he groaned in appreciation.

"God, that's amazing. What on earth is this? It tastes better than it smells, and it smells fabulous."

He chewed his chocolate as Joci peeked into the box, clearly loving what she was smelling.

"Truffles. My favorite chocolate truffles. Aren't they amazing?"

Gunnar swallowed his truffle and handed the box to his mom. "You've got to try one. You'll never eat anything better than that. Thanks, Molly."

Molly smiled her most brilliant smile as the box was passed around to each person in the room.

"Jeez, these are great. Wow, Molly, you've been keeping secrets from us," JT teased.

She nodded. "Well, I told you these were for special occasions, and this is the first special occasion I've been invited to with you all."

Gunnar stood up and said, "I'll be right back." Gunnar walked out to his truck and came back in with a box.

"Mom, since today I officially leave my old name behind, I thought tonight we could look through this box. There are some pictures in it of people I don't know and thought you could help me with them."

Joci looked at the box and wrinkled her nose. "Where did you get them?"

"When Keith died, his wife, Dianna, found some of his things she thought I might want. Connor brought it over yesterday." Keith was Gunnar's biological father, and by the stench coming from the box, he was also a heavy smoker.

Connor was Keith's best friend and had professed his love to Joci, which Jeremiah hated. But Connor had always been there for her and Gunnar, and Jeremiah understood; he hated it, but he understood.

Gunnar sat down and opened the box on the coffee table. He pulled some pictures from the box and laid them on the table and set the box on the floor. The picture on top was one of Keith and Joci when they were much younger. Gunnar looked so much like Keith; it was uncanny. When Gunnar had met him at the hospital after Joci's accident, he looked like a decrepit old man. His hair was thin and of no color, his skin was ashy from the chemo and other drugs. He was a shell of the man he had once been.

There was a picture of Keith on his motorcycle, and a few pictures of Keith with another woman—all being thumbed through and passed around on the table.

"Hey, that's my mom."

Everyone looked at Molly with furrowed brows. Molly pointed to a picture of Keith with her mom—the other woman.

Joci's eyes widened as she took a closer look at the picture. She looked up at Molly with such surprise on her face.

"Your mom is Tori?"

Everyone looked at Molly with indescribable expressions on their faces. Molly swallowed hard and nodded slowly.

Joci looked back at the picture and then back up at Molly. She looked at Jeremiah and then slowly looked at Gunnar.

"Is Keith your father?"

Gunnar's head snapped to attention. He looked at Molly as her face flamed a bright red. JT hissed out "holy fuck" and Jeremiah and Ryder were stone silent.

Ryder put his arm around Molly, hugging her tightly. "It's okay, Molly."

Molly's voice was weak. "I don't know who my biological father is. While my mom was pregnant, he left her."

"Sounds like Keith," Joci commented as she looked back and forth between Molly and Gunnar. How could she have not seen that before? They looked so much alike now that she saw them in this light.

"Gunnar, sit next to Molly, please?" Joci asked.

JT moved over, and Gunnar sat next to her. You could have heard a pin drop.

Jeremiah was the first to find his voice. "I'll be damned; would you look at that?"

Same hair, same eyes, same mouth, same coloring. They looked like brother and sister.

"How old are you Molly?" Joci asked.

"Twenty-four. I'll be twenty-five in January."

Joci began counting. Gunnar was born in May. He was two months old when Joci caught Keith and Tori together. If Molly were born in January, Tori would have already been pregnant in June. She would have been newly pregnant when she was in the delivery room with Joci.

"Then your mom married someone else?"

Molly swallowed the lump in her throat. "Yes. Before I was born, she married my stepdad."

∽

C ould Molly be more mortified? She doubted it. She still wasn't up to speed with everyone else, but what she was getting out of this conversation is that Gunnar could be her biological brother. Her mom had told her that she had cheated on her best friend with her biological father.

She swallowed the large lump in her throat and explained. "One time when I had asked my mom about my biological father, she had told me that she loved him so much that she was willing to give up the friendship of her best friend for him. She knew it was wrong, but she had fallen head-over-heels for him, that he was her world. When he found out she was pregnant, he dumped her and took off. She had told me to forget about him, that he wasn't worth my time or attention."

Her head began to spin, the heat crawled up her body, heating her chest and cheeks. "She never told me I had a biological brother."

"Where is your mom now, Molly?" Joci needed to know if this was what she thought it was. For certain, Gunnar and Molly needed to know if they were biological siblings—half-siblings—but brother and sister just the same.

"She's in a nursing home. She started drinking when I was about eleven. She drank...a lot. A few years ago she had a stroke, and she's never fully recovered. She remembers some days, but most days she doesn't. I've tried asking her again about my biological father, but she won't talk about him." Molly looked at her fingers as she twisted them in her lap.

Almost whispering, Molly continued, "She said she'd never forgiven herself for cheating on her best friend with him. Was that you, Joci?"

"Yes. It was me. She cheated with Keith, Gunnar's biological father."

They continued looking at the pictures as Molly sat completely still. She was afraid to move or breathe or do anything. Joci and her whole family must certainly hate her now. She *was* a terrible person, born of two cheaters. What kind of person could she ever be with genes like that?

"I would like to go and see her," Joci said, looking at Molly.

Jeremiah wrapped his arm around Joci's shoulders and kissed the side of her head.

"Baby, is that a good idea with you being pregnant? You've had such a hard time of it. Please don't put extra stress on yourself or the baby."

Joci looked at Jeremiah and smiled at him. She kissed him on the lips and touched the side of his face.

"If Gunnar and Molly are biological siblings, they have the right to know. Since Tori married someone else before Molly was born, his name would be listed on her birth certificate. The only person that might be able to confirm who Molly's father is would be Tori. They could have blood tests completed, but this could save them that if Tori can speak to us about it."

Joci looked at Molly and Gunnar. "How do you two feel about it?"

Molly sat quietly, waiting for Gunnar's reaction. Gunnar looked down at Molly and lightly nudged her with his shoulder. "I want to know. Do you?"

Tears stung her eyes. "Don't you all hate me?" She looked around at each of them. Joci got up and walked around and kneeled right in front of her. She took Molly's hands in hers and looked her right in the eye.

"Why would we hate you? You're not responsible for the sins of your parents. Look around you at these people in this room. JT and Ryder have Jeremiah, but their biological mother is a nightmare. Sorry, boys." Joci looked at JT and Ryder. They just smiled at her and nodded.

"Gunnar's father, who is quite possibly your father, was certainly a nightmare. My parents were great but died when I was very young. I was left to my own devices with my sister, which is what drove me to Keith in the first place. Each of us has things to overcome. Look at you. You've turned out fantastic in spite of your parentage. We do not hate you, Molly. We all love you. My son loves you most of all."

Molly burst into tears and wrapped her arms around Joci's shoulders. Her feelings were all over the board. My God, she was fortunate to find these people. Little did she know years ago when she met Joci just how deeply their lives would intersect.

Joci hugged Molly for a long while, patting and rubbing soothing circles across her back. When Molly was able to pull herself together, Joci framed Molly's face in her hands and wiped the tears away with her thumbs. "Now. Do you think we can go and see your mom? I want to see if she can remember."

Molly nodded. "We can try and see if she'll remember. Most days she's not very cooperative."

Joci looked at Gunnar. "Are you okay with this, honey?"

Gunnar smirked. "Yeah. In one day I gained a dad, two brothers, and a sister. How many people get to say that?"

# 14

## TORI

On the way home, Molly stared out the window of the truck, lost in thought. Now that Ryder knew that she might be Gunnar's sister, did he think differently of her? It was a strange situation. Strange—hell, it was downright impossible to dream up stuff like this. She had known Joci for about six years now and never—in either of their dreams—would they have ever thought something like this.

Ryder pulled the truck into the garage and closed the door. He opened his door and noticed that Molly hadn't moved.

"Hey. You still with me?"

She shook her head once and blinked a couple of times. "Yeah. Sorry. I'm coming."

She stepped out of the truck and walked around to the kitchen door. Ryder stood there waiting for her. He wrapped his arms around her and pulled her close. She could feel his warmth seep into her. Hearing him breathe in her scent, she closed her eyes and soaked up his love and strength.

"I love you, Molly. Nothing will change that."

She looked up at him. "Are you sure? This is pretty weird, you know. Most men would run screaming and yelling from me as fast as they could."

"Well, most men are stupid. At least, that's what we're always told," he said, smirking at her.

She giggled. "Well. That's true."

Ryder bent down and smacked her on the ass as he opened the door and gently pushed her inside.

"We should wait to tell them you're moving in; don't you think?"

"Yeah. Let's tackle one thing at a time. It doesn't change anything anyway. I'm usually here all the time, so it's just a matter of moving the remainder of my clothes and my bike here. A few other things, but nothing I need immediately."

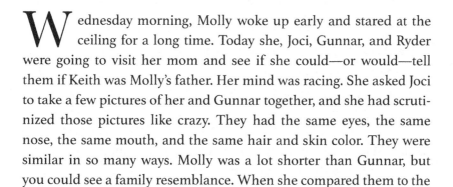

Wednesday morning, Molly woke up early and stared at the ceiling for a long time. Today she, Joci, Gunnar, and Ryder were going to visit her mom and see if she could—or would—tell them if Keith was Molly's father. Her mind was racing. She asked Joci to take a few pictures of her and Gunnar together, and she had scrutinized those pictures like crazy. They had the same eyes, the same nose, the same mouth, and the same hair and skin color. They were similar in so many ways. Molly was a lot shorter than Gunnar, but you could see a family resemblance. When she compared them to the pictures of Keith, she definitely saw that they all looked alike.

She had grown up without siblings but had always dreamed of having a brother or sister. Gunnar told her he had felt the same way, and now, here they were, possibly siblings. Would it be too late to build a bond? She'd felt a connection with Gunnar the first time they'd met. It was nothing romantic at all, but a kinship that she couldn't describe. Gunnar told her he had felt it as well when they had lunch together yesterday.

"A penny for your thoughts."

Molly looked over at Ryder. He was lying on his side with his head in his hand, staring at her. He was still the most handsome man she'd ever met. Her tummy still did flip-flops when she saw him walk in the door at night after work. Her breath still stuttered when he kissed her. And the sex—well, there were no words for the feel of him sliding inside her.

"I bet you would want it back if you knew." She sighed.

She slowly pushed Ryder to his back and crawled on top of him, kissing his neck, his jaw, his mouth. Oh, she loved this man.

Ryder grabbed Molly's ass in both hands and pushed her down on top of his quickly growing erection.

"You better not be thinking about our brother. I'm going to start getting jealous of all the time you spend thinking about him."

*Our brother*. He had begun saying that a lot. It was weird, yet it was more than likely true.

"Who *should* I be thinking about?" she whispered, pecking soft kisses on his jaw.

"Hmm. Maybe you should think about me. Think about how it feels when my tongue slides along your cute little pussy, how it dips inside of you to get a taste. Think about how it feels when I slide myself inside of you. When I suck on your hard little nipples and make you come."

"Hmm. That does sound nice. But..."

Within seconds, Ryder had Molly rolled onto her back looking up at him. He shoved himself quickly inside of her and pulled all the way out. She moaned at the loss of him inside. He rubbed his swollen cock on her clit and pushed down, grinding around a few times. She watched his pupils dilate and his nostrils flare. He pushed inside of her again, stroked twice, and then pulled all the way out. She groaned again, but he kept himself away from her, so their bodies weren't touching—there. She grabbed his hips and tried pulling him down on top of her, but he was stronger. She whimpered and tried pushing her pelvis up to touch him, but she couldn't reach.

He smiled down at her. "What are you thinking about now, babe?"

"Gah, this is frustrating. I'm thinking about you." She tugged on his hips to bring him closer to her.

"Yeah? What are you thinking about me?"

"Ryder, please." She squirmed.

"Since you asked so nicely." He slid inside of her again, stroking in and out a few times. He pulled himself all the way out again and kissed her thoroughly and hungrily. He fell to his elbows and rubbed against her a few times. Her hips pushed up into him, seeking release. He smiled down at her. "What are you doing, Molly?"

"Ryder, please. I need to come."

He chuckled. "I need a condom. Hang on, babe."

"No, you don't. I went on the pill a couple of weeks ago. Please, Ryder —I need you."

"Did you now?"

"Yes. I wanted to feel you inside of me without a condom."

He looked at her, his smile devastating. His lips glistened from kissing her and the green in his eyes glimmered as a ray of light through the window captured him, illuminating his features. He slowly dipped his head and nipped at her bottom lip while he leisurely entered her. She moaned; he felt like heaven.

~

Ryder pumped in and out a few times and reached down to hook Molly's leg over his arm so he could push deeper into her. God, that was perfect. She was perfect. He stroked in and out in perfect rhythm, grinding himself against her every few strokes.

"Come with me, babe," he husked out.

"Yes," she whispered.

Three more thrusts and she cried out his name as her orgasm rolled over her in wave after wave of sensation. God, he loved the way she made him feel—like there was no one else in this world, nothing else that mattered but him. The way it felt sliding into her bare—well, hell, there were no words. He continued pumping into her as her orgasm continued, then he stiffened and poured himself into her for the first time without a condom. Damn that felt so good. Nope, he'd never wear a condom again.

They giggled as they cleaned up the mess. "I don't care; I loved the feeling of going bareback. I'm never wearing a condom again."

Molly laughed out loud. "Bareback? Is that what it's called?" He nodded and grinned.

They were still for a few minutes. "So, now that we're both feeling relaxed, you want to tell me what you were studying on the ceiling?"

Molly chuckled. "I'm both nervous and excited for today. I still can't believe this is happening. You couldn't write this stuff."

He chuckled. She was right about *that*. Life was certainly stranger than fiction—or something like that.

He pulled Molly into his arms and held on to her, kissed the top of her head and rubbed his hand up and down her arm. Breathing in her scent, he squeezed her gently, going over his question in his mind.

"Are you embarrassed about me meeting your mom?" he finally asked.

Molly lifted up so she could look into his eyes. "No. Do I seem like I am?" Her brows furrowed. "I never want you to feel that way. I love you...more than anything, I hope you can understand that she's not...well."

Ryder shook his head. "Don't worry; I get it. I understand. You haven't met *my* mother yet—my biological mother. You'll see *not well*."

They both chuckled.

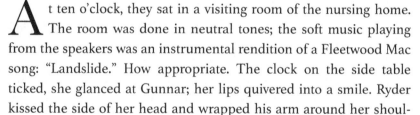

At ten o'clock, they sat in a visiting room of the nursing home. The room was done in neutral tones; the soft music playing from the speakers was an instrumental rendition of a Fleetwood Mac song: "Landslide." How appropriate. The clock on the side table ticked, she glanced at Gunnar; her lips quivered into a smile. Ryder kissed the side of her head and wrapped his arm around her shoulders. Joci smiled and reached forward from the chair she sat in to pat her hand.

The door opened, and a nurse walked in pushing Tori in a wheelchair. She wheeled her over to the table and locked the wheels on the chair. The nurse looked at Molly. "Do you want me to stay, hon?"

Molly's lips turned down in a frown as she took in her mother's appearance. In her youth, she'd been a pretty woman with soft brown hair and brown eyes. Sitting here looking at her today, that pretty woman was no longer present. Her eyes were the dull gaze of a person who merely existed in the body, the light dimmed. Her hair, where it had once been thick and full, was now a drab gray and hung limply to her shoulders in a lifeless bob. Her pretty, clear complexion was muddy—her skin now blotchy from the medications she took. Once in a while, some of it would come back; a light would go on, but it would always go back off.

"Maybe you better in case she has a tantrum," Molly said as she slowly stood.

The nurse nodded. Leaning down to look into Tori's eyes, she said, "Ms. Elson, I will be right here if you need me." Tori didn't respond, just sat staring at the table in front of her. The nurse took a chair in the corner.

Molly looked at the others. "Sometimes she gets upset that she can't remember things. Or maybe that she can't remember me and throws tantrums, probably out of frustration. They're not sure." She glanced back to her mom.

They nodded and stood to move to the table. Tori glanced up as Joci approached her and she cocked her head. Joci smiled at her and said, "Hello Tori. How are you?"

Tori's lips trembled and slightly turned up at the ends, but her attention diverted to Gunnar who had claimed a chair next to her. Tori squealed, "Keith, you came to see me! I've been waiting so long for you."

Tori grabbed Gunnar's hand and held on for dear life. Gunnar looked at his mom and then at Molly.

"Mom. This isn't Keith; this is Gunnar."

"Gunnar? No, Gunnar's a baby. I was with Joci when she had him. It scared the hell out of me watching her deliver. I'm going to have a baby, and I don't want to go through that."

Well, that was easy. Summed up what they came here for. Joci looked at Tori still holding Gunnar's hand.

"Joci. Oh, Joci, how are you? I'm so sorry, Joci. Please don't be mad at me."

Tori began to cry, tears flooding her dull eyes. She wiped her eyes and nose with her hands, and the nurse came over to wipe her hands with a moist cloth and gave her a tissue.

"Tori, is your baby Keith's baby?"

"I can't tell you. I'm not supposed to say anything. Keith said if I told you, he would leave me."

Tori looked at Gunnar. "Tell her Keith, tell her what you told me."

Gunnar looked at his mom and raised his eyebrows. He turned to Molly and mouthed *sorry*.

"Tori, are you pregnant with my baby?"

"Yes, Keith, I told you. I'm due in January. We're going to have a baby."

Tori smiled as she looked into Gunnar's eyes. She continued to hold his hands in hers and leaned down and kissed his fingers. Gunnar's spine stiffened as he watched her face. She was clearly lost in another world, twenty-five years back. Was that the last time she was truly happy? So sad to think she had lived a miserable life all these years. Keith sure screwed up a lot of people. Some people make it through; some crack under the pressure.

Joci spoke up first. "It's not definitive, but I would bet my life on it by looking at you two. I didn't know anyone else that Tori saw back then. She certainly could have been pregnant with Molly when I delivered Gunnar. She always told me when she was seeing someone. Except for Keith, of course."

Molly looked around the table and saw that everyone had the information they were looking for; there was no need to stay any longer.

Tori didn't know Molly. She lived in the past most the time and Molly didn't exist in the past.

Molly turned to the nurse. "Thank you. We'll take off then."

Gunnar started to stand up, but Tori held his hands tight. She began crying in earnest, the tears flowing freely down her cheeks. "Please don't leave me, Keith. I didn't tell her; I promise I didn't."

Well, now it was just uncomfortable. Gunnar crouched down in front of Tori and took both of her hands in his. "Tori, I have to go to work, but I'll come back as soon as I can, okay?"

"Okay." Tori's crooked smile showed yellowed teeth. The nurse stepped in and wiped her eyes and nose. Without a word, she unlocked the wheels on Tori's wheelchair and quickly ushered her away. Molly took a deep breath and watched her mother glide out the door.

Turning to the others, she said, "They get her out quickly without a lot of preamble; it's easier when they take her back to her room. When I first started coming to visit, it was gut-wrenching leaving her; I used to cry and so would she. But they told me it upset my mom so much that she wouldn't eat for days and she had a hard time with her temper." She glanced at the door and clenched her fists tightly. "So now when I come to visit, we say a few words and the nurses quickly pull her away and get her to her room. She's probably already forgotten she had visitors."

"Has she always lived in the past like this?" Joci asked, her brows furrowed. "I feel so sad for her, for the life she's living, and she clearly has a difficult time coping."

Molly's lips formed a straight line. "Yes. She drank a lot after she and my stepfather divorced. She was trying to forget...things." She tucked her hair behind her ear. "Anyway, she had a stroke and has been like this since that day. The stroke shoved her into the past, and she doesn't seem to want to remember anything else."

Ryder watched Molly. His stomach twisted in knots just watching her and seeing the sadness on her face. At least he had his dad, his grandma, and now Joci. "Molly, who does your mom think you are?" he asked.

She shook her head. "I don't know. She used to call me Nancy. Now, she doesn't address me with a name or seem to think I'm anyone."

"Keith's mom's name is Nancy," Joci thought out loud. The kids all looked at her. Joci caught Molly's gaze and smiled. "She had the dark hair and blue eyes."

When Joci stood up, the others followed suit. It was clearly time to go.

On the ride home, Ryder looked over at Molly. "Why is your last name Bates and your mom's last name is Elson?"

Molly closed her eyes. She took a deep breath and let it out slowly.

"Hey. You with me?" He glanced at her and then to the road.

She swallowed. "Yes. I'm with you."

When she didn't say anything further, he lifted an eyebrow at her and cocked his head to the side.

She took a deep breath, then slowly exhaled. "I changed my name when I was thirteen."

"Why would you do that?" he asked.

A single tear slid down Molly's face. "I didn't want to be known as Molly Elson anymore. Lancaster Elson was my stepfather, and I didn't want his last name. I didn't know who my biological father was, so I chose Bates."

"Why didn't you want to keep Elson?" He pulled into the garage and put the truck in park.

"I couldn't. He wasn't my father." Her fingers twisted in her sweater, her voice cracked.

He looked at her skeptically, reached over to hold her hand and gave it a squeeze. He would eventually find out what she was hiding from him.

## 15

# THE ANNIVERSARY

November fifteenth was the Sheppard matriarchs'—Thomas and Emily's—fiftieth wedding anniversary. Since the fifteenth was on Wednesday, they waited until the weekend to celebrate. They were having a party at a hall just outside of Green Bay. With Emily's guidance, the daughters-in-law had done most of the planning. Not only would all the kids and grandkids be there, but Emily and Thomas' siblings and friends would be there as well. Molly was about to meet the whole Sheppard family. Of course, the faces would look familiar to her because they were at Jeremiah and Joci's wedding. But meeting them as Ryder's girlfriend—as well as Gunnar's sister—was a whole different matter. She was nervous as a cat. She'd always feared being judged for things that had happened in the past, especially those things she'd had no control over. Would they think less of her?

"You're a beautiful woman, Molly Bates," Ryder said as he walked over and tucked his notebook in the top drawer of the dresser. Molly watched him turn and walk toward her.

She smiled and looked up at him in the mirror in front of her. She had a new dress on and was trying to decide if it was too tight to wear.

The impression she wanted to make was not that of a hoochie momma. The fitted fuchsia, sleeveless dress with black lace over the top and a skinny black belt around the waist came to her knees, but it made her look sleek and sexy. Her black strappy, high-heeled shoes finished her outfit.

"You're beautiful yourself, Ryder Sheppard. You clean up nice." She had purchased black dress pants, a black dress shirt with tiny fuchsia pinstripes in it, and a fuchsia tie for him.

He grinned, and all she could do was stare at him. She meant it; he was beautiful—so very beautiful—inside and out. This past week they had learned so many things about each other—mostly revelations about Molly and her past, but she learned things about Ryder, too. He was patient, kind, and he didn't judge her or her mom. He was loyal to those he loved and thoughtful, always making sure Molly was taken care of. She couldn't love anyone more.

"When are you going to tell me what you keep writing in that notebook?" She smiled.

He turned her around to face him. Laying his hands on her shoulders, he stepped back and looked her up and down. Damn, she was fine—so fine. Every time he looked at her, he was again struck by how lucky he'd been to have found her. He had found out a lot about this woman these past months. She had a mother who didn't even know who she was. She had friends who loved her and cared for her. She was talented, beautiful, and loving, in spite of the hand life had dealt her. He loved her more than he had ever dreamed he could love anyone.

"Nice dress, babe. I'm going to have to fight the men off tonight for sure." One side of his mouth hitched up in a cocky grin.

She laughed. "You're so dramatic. And considering most of the men will be in their seventies, I don't think you have anything to worry about. But, thank you. You don't think it's too...sexy or tight, do you?"

"I think it's perfect."

She kissed him softly, swiping her tongue across his lips twice, making him groan and pull her in tight to his body. He held her head in his hands and continued kissing her until he needed air. He wrapped his arms around her and held her close, breathing in her scent and enjoying the feel of her against his body.

She reached down between them and rubbed his already growing erection. "I love the way you feel when you're hard for me, Ryder. It's so damn sexy." She sighed.

"I'm always hard for you, Molly. Tell me what you have on under that damn sexy dress so I can think about it all night. Do you have that sweet little black lacy thong on?"

She giggled. "I do have a black lacy thong on, but it's a new one. I couldn't find my other one."

"Mmm, a new one. Sweet. I'll be hard all night thinking about taking it off of you."

He kissed her again and swatted her on the butt. "We have to get going, babe."

"So, you're going to just avoid talking about the notebook?"

Ryder smiled. "For now."

He walked out toward the living room to wait for Molly to finish getting ready. If he stayed in the bedroom with her any longer, they would soon be undressed. Just thinking about her little black thong made his cock swell and his heart beat faster. He couldn't wait to get home, undress her, and sink balls deep into her tight little pussy. Damn, he was addicted to her.

They arrived at the hall around six-thirty, just as his cousins, Mark and Mike, Thomas and Erin's boys, were walking in. They greeted each other with handshakes and hugs and Ryder re-introduced them to Molly. They went in to get drinks from the bar and joined the family members who had already arrived.

Ryder introduced Molly to each person as they were greeted. He was so damn proud to introduce her to his family. Her full lips parted into a smile as she met each family member. The blue in her eyes seemed more pronounced with the pink of her dress. And the heels, shit, those made her legs look long and lean and so damn sexy.

Following dinner, Thomas and Emily gave speeches as the band softly played dance music in the background. When the speeches were over, he leaned into her and whispered in her ear, "Dance with me." It was a command and a request at the same time.

"Aren't you worried your family will watch us?" she questioned.

"Not at all." He whispered in her ear as he pulled her close. "They'll be happy to see me happy." He twirled her into the middle of the floor and pulled her close again. "You make me happy."

She wrapped her arms around his shoulders and tucked her head on his shoulder. She was breathy when she spoke. "Wow, Ryder, you're a great dancer. How'd you learn?"

He chuckled. "Growing up, I had a friend, Matt. Matt loved acting in the school plays. He talked me into trying out for a couple of parts with him. They were always musicals, and the school had a dance coach come in and show us some steps for the plays." He spun her tightly as he held her close. "He said we would be happy we learned the basics. I guess he was right."

He bent his head so the sides of their faces were touching as they continued to sway to the music. He was definitely under a spell, swaying to the soft music, Molly in his arms.

Around eleven-thirty, they walked into her house. She leaned down to pull her shoes off and groaned a little when her feet flatly hit the floor.

"I don't understand how women wear those shoes. But...your legs look amazing in them, so I'm not complaining." He kissed her lips.

She chuckled. "Sometimes I don't know why I wear them, either."

Then she saucily stated, "I don't understand how a man can walk around with a hard rod between his legs for an entire evening. It must get painful."

He grinned. "Fuck yeah, but now you can ease my pain and make it all worthwhile."

He scooped her up into his arms and carried her to the bedroom, setting her down so her feet were on the floor, kissed her softly, then took a step back.

"We're going to play a game tonight. Are you in?"

"What kind of game?" she asked apprehensively.

"Nope. You don't get to ask before you agree. You're either in with me or not. What'll it be?"

~

S he looked at the desire on his face. It could only be good. And she'd been serious before; he'd had a hard-on all night long. She felt it pushing into her belly as they danced. This little game could only end in both of them being pleasured.

"Okay. I'm in."

Ryder smiled, the sight robbing her of breath. He held up his index finger, silently telling her to wait a minute. He turned on the little lamp on the dresser and turned off the overhead light. He lit two candles on either side of the bed and walked over to stand in front of her once again.

"Here's how it goes. We'll take turns. First me, then you. I get to undress you, kiss you, touch you, do anything I want to you and you have to stand there and let me. You are not allowed to touch me in return until it's your turn. Understand?"

She raised her brows. "Yes."

He smirked, lifted his hand and ran the backs of his fingers down her cheek. He flipped his hand, lightly grazing her skin, along her jaw, down to her neck and around to the nape. His eyes never left hers. He leaned his head down and kissed her lips—softly at first. As his kiss became more insistent and greedy, she opened for him and let his tongue slide in and taste her. She moaned as the breath escaped her lungs, and Ryder hummed as he caught it in his mouth.

She reached her arms up to hold on to his head, but Ryder pulled away.

"If you touch me, I'll stop. That means I'll stop pleasuring you and then it will be your turn to pleasure me."

Since Molly wasn't ready to give up her pleasure, she brought her arms down to her sides. She would exact her revenge on him when it was her turn.

He smirked and began kissing and licking down her neck, alternating between his lips and tongue. He kissed up her neck to her ear, licking the shell of her ear. She closed her eyes, reveling in the feel of him.

Close to her ear, he whispered, "I love you, Molly."

She smiled and decided to play his game and not say anything until it was her turn to pleasure him.

He slowly slid his hands behind her and unzipped her dress. He pulled the back open and pulled the dress forward and off of her shoulders. Peeling the front down, he hissed out a breath as her full breasts came into view. They were still covered by a little lacy black bra, but good lord, they were magnificent. He gently ran his fingers along the swell and dipped a finger in the valley between them.

"Perfect. You're perfect."

She looked up into his eyes as a soft smiled played on her lips. His nostrils flared, and his breathing became shallow as his fingers slipped over her breasts again and then floated to her back, unhooking her bra, allowing her breasts to spill forward into his hands. He let her bra fall off her shoulders and drop to the floor.

He kissed and licked his way down to her breasts, sucked in a hard nipple and heard Molly exhale as he did. He smiled, amazed she had this much control. He'd been whispering sweet words in her ears all night while they danced—promises of what was to come."

Sometimes she would mewl, sometimes her breath caught in her throat, and twice she begged him to take her home right then and sweetly torture her. He knew she was ready to come, but still, she allowed him to play his game.

He dropped to his knees in front of her and slowly peeled the dress down her hips. He kissed her belly, ringing her navel with his tongue and dipping it inside. She raised her hands, hesitated and let them fall to her sides again. He chuckled, knowing she was waging a war in her head, between wanting more and wanting to touch him. It thrilled him beyond belief, thinking she needed to feel him.

When the dress fell to the floor, he reached up and took her hand. "I'll let you touch me, only to assist you in getting your dress all the way off."

She took his hand to steady herself and stepped out of her dress. He licked and kissed his way down from her navel to the top of her panties. Rocking back on his heels, he admired her from this angle. Looking up at her, viewing her full breasts from this angle was hot. He leaned up and licked the underside of one of them and heard her groan. He grinned. He'd been so close to her pussy; no doubt she wanted his mouth there. But this sweet, slow pleasuring was just too enjoyable to rush through.

"Frustrated, babe? Want my mouth on you? You can tell me; you just can't touch me. Where do you want my mouth baby?"

"Ryder. You're killing me here. Please...lick my pussy. Please."

He chuckled and slipped his fingers into her panties. As he pulled them down her hips, he made sure his fingers grazed along the lips of her pussy, almost making her knees buckle. He chuckled a little more.

"I can see your torture, Molly. Your body is quivering."

He swiped his finger along the seam of her pussy, watching her eyes while he did. "Look at this." Holding up the finger that just swiped along her lips, he smiled. "My finger is dripping with your honey. You're so wet, Molly."

He dipped his head forward and licked her opening, causing Molly to groan loudly and pant. Just two licks and he sat back, making her sound out in frustration.

"Hold my hand, sweetheart, while you step out of your panties."

She held his hand again and stepped out of her panties. He stood and looked into her eyes, smiling at her when she frowned. She clearly wanted him lower. He chuckled and grabbed her around the waist, gently pushing her back until her legs touched the bed.

"I don't want you falling. Now, sit back and keep your sweet, dripping pussy on the edge of the bed. If you want, you can lie back, but you still can't touch me."

She sat on the very edge of the bed, watching Ryder as he watched her. He kneeled down before her again and pushed her legs open with his hands. When her legs spread apart before him, he leaned forward and swiped her pussy with his tongue and then gently blew on the wet trail he left. She mewled, and his cock throbbed; he loved that sound.

He slid two fingers gently inside of her, causing her to groan and quiver. She fell back onto the bed, lacking the strength to hold herself up any longer. He pushed his fingers inside and pulled them slowly out, watching intently as his hands gave Molly pleasure. The only sounds in the room were their raspy breathing and the wet sounds his fingers made sliding in and out of her.

Molly fisted the comforter on the bed, a slight sheen of sweat on her skin and her breath coming out in raspy, ragged pants. Her legs quivered while her pussy was sweetly tormented with his fingers and tongue as he gently licked and sucked her clit.

"Ryder," she panted.

He added a little more pressure to her clit with his tongue, pulled his fingers out and replaced them with his mouth, fucking her with his tongue.

He whispered, "You taste magnificent, Molly—like sweet honey."

He guided his fingers back into her pussy and began a faster rhythm than before. Faster and faster his fingers plundered into her while his tongue started on her clit once more. He worked her up quickly, wanting and needing her release more than his own. He wanted to make her come, to make her feel good, to know he could do that for her. The erotic sounds in the room had him so fucking on edge; he could come with just the touch of her hand on his throbbing cock.

"Ryder!" She cried out his name as her orgasm hit her like the force of a hurricane—quivering and shaking, she continued to moan.

"I'm changing the rules of the game for now. I can't wait a second longer for you. You'll have to exact your revenge later."

He quickly stood, releasing his cock from the confines of his pants. He pulled it out and pushed the broad head to Molly's wet, quivering opening and pushed in hard. She cried out as she felt him push in, not even registering yet what was happening. As she regained her composure, she smiled up at him and raised her legs and wrapped them around his waist as he stood before her, plunging deeply inside of her. Sweat formed on his brow and his face. He was still fully dressed except for his cock.

Ryder grabbed her legs and pulled them from his waist and pushed her knees forward and toward her chest. He smiled at her and began pumping his hard length into her, faster and faster.

"Hold your knees, Molly. Don't let go."

She immediately complied, happy to have something to hang onto. He reached down between them and applied the perfect amount of pressure to her clit, circling his fingers around in seamless rhythm, watching her face.

"Come...come now," his voice raspy, holding on to his orgasm until she reached hers.

She hit the wall and exploded once again just as Ryder pushed hard into her and held as his hot juices spurt into Molly's body. Stream after stream flowed from his cock; he thought he would never stop coming. After what seemed like an eternity, he fell forward as she let go of her knees and opened her legs for him to fall on top of her. She wrapped her arms around his back and hung on.

# 16

## THE HOUSE

The end of November was busy; the bikes were put away for the winter. Ryder still hadn't officially moved in with Molly. With the commotion over Molly and Gunnar being brother and sister, they decided to keep things as they were for a while. But they were meeting with a banker today to draw up an Offer to Purchase, and hopefully Jeffrey Jepson would sign it. Molly was nervous thinking about Jepson and hoped he wouldn't back out or decide he wanted more money for the house. They had the paper from Mr. Jepson, but it wasn't a binding contract so Jeffrey could easily change his mind. If they had to go by the appraisal, it would cost them a lot more. They could still make it happen, but they had some changes they wanted to make to the house, and any additional cost would delay those changes.

They spent time loving each other and getting to know each other better. More than once they'd gone out with Ryder's family to The Barn. Rachel was usually there and always incredibly rude to Molly. She thought nothing of touching and grabbing Ryder and letting her know—several times—that they'd had sex, and it was amazing. Molly tried to ignore her; Rachel meant nothing to Ryder, and she knew that.

Molly pulled her favorite coffee cups—the kind with chalkboard paint so you can write messages—from the cupboard and poured coffee for herself and Ryder. There was little better in the world than the smell of fresh caramel coffee. She added creamer to hers and stirred. A thud sounded from the front of the house. Ryder was in the shower, so she knew it wasn't him. She padded into the living room and looked out the large front window. The street was empty and quiet. As the weather had turned cooler, the neighbors began tucking themselves away indoors. She shrugged, stepped into the kitchen and in blue chalk drew a heart on Ryder's cup. Smiling, she picked up their cups and strode back to the bedroom and waited for him to finish showering.

Ryder walked into the bedroom with a towel draped around his hips. Gawd, he was so dreamy. His tight abs still glistened from his shower as they angled to narrow hips with his happy trail pointing the way to Molly's playground. She grinned as she looked him up and down. Settling on the later, she licked her lips. The towel twitched, and Molly raised an eyebrow.

"That thing has a mind of its own."

"Well, when you look at me like you want it, it naturally responds to you. Not my fault, babe."

She laughed and handed Ryder his cup of coffee. He winked at her, looked at the heart and stepped into her for a kiss. "I love you, too." He turned and walked to the closet to get dressed.

She pulled off her robe and began gathering her clothes to take a shower. She pulled out her favorite blue lacy bra and rummaged around in her drawer for the matching blue lace panties. Ryder stepped up behind her and wrapped his arms around her waist.

With his mouth close to her ear, he said, "And now you stand here completely naked, and you don't want my cock to get excited? With that perfect ass of yours rubbing against me, I could come right now." He ground against her a couple of times and the feel of his cock becoming rigid sent a shiver down her arms.

She turned in his arms and wrapped her arms around his neck. Wiggling against his cock, she nipped at his earlobe. He groaned and tightened his hold on her; she chuckled.

"Well, I was looking for my matching panties, but you've just made an excellent case for not wearing them."

"Perfect—go without panties today. When I get home, I want you ready for me to ravish you completely. I'll only be gone a couple of hours; then we'll go to the bank, and afterward, we'll play some more."

She kissed his jaw, down his neck and across his chest. When she reached his dragon tattoo, she licked it and heard him suck in his breath. He just did it for her. His scent was tantalizing; those eyes of his looked at her like she was the only woman in the world for him and that excited her beyond reason. He'd grown bolder with her, and she loved it. Sexually, he was an amazing, demanding lover and exhausted her daily. Still, she couldn't get enough of him.

He slid his hand into her hair and fisted it, so he had a firm grip on her. "Continue and I won't wait until I get home."

Molly smiled up at him. Sliding her hand down his abdomen, she grabbed his cock as it strained against the rough fabric of his jeans. She could feel the hardness just beneath, and her breathing grew ragged. Just the thought of him not being able to wait any longer made her wet.

With a groan, Ryder quickly turned Molly away from him and bent her over the dresser she had just been rummaging in. She smiled as she looked up at him in the mirror. He returned her smile and slowly slid his fingers down the seam of her ass, ringing her puckered little nub and continuing down to the slick entrance of her pussy.

When he felt her wetness, he hissed out a breath. "Fuck, Molly, you're so wet for me. Do you know what that does to me, knowing how wet you get when I touch you?"

She couldn't do anything but moan as he continued sliding his fingers inside and pulling out to slide them over her clit and then back into her quivering wetness. She looked down at the dresser and gripped the edge to keep her balance.

"No, Molly, look at me. Don't take your eyes off of mine, do you hear me?"

She nodded. "No, say it. I want to hear it."

Swallowing, she said, "I'll keep my eyes on you."

"Good girl. Now, I'm going to take you hard and fast; do you understand me?"

"Yes." It was barely a whisper. She was so turned on right now her legs shook. Good thing she was leaning over the dresser. She heard the zipper on his jeans and the rustle as he pushed them down his thighs, but he never took his eyes from hers. Gah! The waiting was maddening. She was so fucking hot; she couldn't even take a full breath. When she whimpered, he smirked at her in the mirror.

"Is it hard waiting for it, Molly? Are you about ready to come just thinking about my cock sliding inside of you?"

Molly whimpered again. God, yes. If he continued speaking to her like that, she probably would come.

"I'm going to slide inside of you quickly. I want you to think about this all day."

Ryder touched the puckered little opening to her ass and added a little pressure. He didn't breach her entrance, but he could see her excitement and smiled at her in the mirror.

He leaned down and whispered in her ear, "Tonight, I'm going to be in you right here. Your tight little ass is going to squeeze my hard cock so tight that I won't be able to think straight. Do you understand me?"

Geez, one more word—just one—and she was going to explode. She watched his beautiful green eyes as he watched her reaction. She couldn't look away if she wanted to.

"Yes." It was all she could say.

She felt the broad head of Ryder's cock touch her wet pussy and push in just the barest little bit.

"Hard and fast, okay?"

"Yes."

"Touch yourself—make yourself come with me."

Ryder thrust up into Molly hard. She moaned at the feeling, so damn good. With his hands on her hips, he began thrusting hard and fast into her body. He was careful not to push her hips into the dresser. He held her firmly with both hands as he continued the glorious assault on her body, pushing harder and faster until it shook her to the core. He grinned at her in the mirror, watching her eyes.

Molly's fingers worked furiously. This was going to be fast.

"Jesus, you feel incredible," he grunted.

Ryder bent his knees to get under her so he could thrust up into her. When he did, Molly pulled her bottom lip between her teeth and moaned.

"Come for me, Molly. Come now; I'm so fucking close."

She called out his name as she stiffened and let her orgasm roll over her whole body. Her breasts, her back, and her forehead wore a light sheen of perspiration. She didn't care; she loved their moments of hot, spontaneous sex when he pounded into her and showed her how much he desired her.

Two thrusts later, Ryder tightened his grip on her hips and let his release flow into her body. He collapsed on her back, his breathing ragged and his body sweating with the exertion. They lay like this for a few minutes, both of them slowly returning to earth. He finally lifted his head and kissed her between her shoulder blades. He pulled out and grabbed a towel from the bathroom to clean them both up. He hadn't even taken his jeans completely off, she'd noticed. *That's so hot.*

"What are you smiling at?" he huffed.

"You. You didn't even wait to get your jeans off. I love that you get so excited for me."

He shook his head. "I feel like an animal with you sometimes. You completely take my common sense and throw it out the window. Sometimes I look at you, and I just have to have you now, even though I would love to wait and make it special."

She turned and stared into his beautiful eyes. Her palm cupped his jaw, her thumb smoothing the soft, supple skin on his lips. "Every time is special with you, Ryder. Don't you understand, you make my self-control fly out the window as well?"

He dipped his head and covered her lips with his, completely devouring her lips, his tongue sliding into her mouth and mating with her tongue. He lifted his head just enough to look into her eyes a moment longer. He lovingly smacked her on the ass. "Gotta go, babe. JT and Gunnar are waiting for me. We won't be long today; it's just the last little bit of work on Danny's place." He grabbed his shirt from the foot of the bed where he'd tossed it and slid it over his head. "Which reminds me, Danny and Tammy wanted to go out with us tomorrow night. Did you and Tammy talk about where and when?"

"Yeah. We thought we could go out for wings and maybe to The Barn or somewhere else afterward. You good with that?"

"Perfect. Love you, see you in a couple of hours."

He tucked his shirt in while Molly watched him walk out of the bedroom. She turned back to the drawer to try and find the blue panties that matched her bra. She couldn't find them anywhere. Oh well, she would have to go without. Ryder wanted her like that anyway. With a sly smile, she walked to the bathroom to shower up and get dressed.

As Molly finished applying her makeup, she heard a knock on the front door. With her brows furrowed while wondering who could be there, she slowly walked to the living room, an uneasy feeling settling deep in her gut. Stupid, why would she feel uncomfortable? But just in case, she peeked out the window next to the front door. Holy shit, Jeffrey Jepson! Crap! Now what? Maybe he wanted to talk about the offer on the house, but she didn't want to be alone with him. Ryder would be gone for another hour or so. As she stood there wondering what to do, another loud rap sounded on the front door.

She quietly padded into the kitchen, picked her cell phone off the counter and tapped Ryder's image.

"Hey babe, what's up?"

"Ryder, Jeffrey Jepson is knocking on the door. I don't know what to do. I don't want to be alone with him, but what if he's here about the house? What should I do?"

Ryder could hear the loud banging over the phone. "Fuck! I'll be right there. Yell out the door and tell him just a minute. I'll call Frank next door and ask him to run over and stay with you until I get there. I saw him outside when I left. Are you okay?"

"Yeah, just a little freaked. It sounds like he's starting to get pissed."

The knocking grew louder, and she heard Jeffrey yell from the other side of the door. "Molly, I want to speak with you."

"Stay on the phone with me, Molly...JT, call Molly's neighbor Frank and ask him to run over to her house and stay with her until I get there. Here's the number... I'm on my way. Did you hear that, Molly? Stay on the phone with me while I'm driving. If you feel like you need to open the door, go ahead, but don't let him in, and keep me on the line."

"Okay."

She slowly walked to the door. Grateful that she had a locked storm door, she opened the main door and held up her finger to Jeffrey Jepson so he could see she was on the phone. He scowled at her, but she continued to talk to Ryder, not saying much, but making it look like she was involved with a customer. Suddenly, Frank was on the doorstep with Jeffrey.

"Ryder, Frank's here now. I'm going to let them in."

"Keep me on the phone, Molly. I want to hear what's going on until I can get there. I'm not far now."

"Okay. I love you."

"I love you too, baby. Don't worry; this will be fine."

She turned toward the door and unlocked the storm door with shaking fingers. "Hello, I was finishing up with a customer...thank you for waiting."

Grateful that her voice didn't sound shaky, she stood aside as Frank and Jeffrey walked in. "Hi Frank, Ryder says he's not far from here, and he's sorry he's late. Can you wait?"

"Absolutely, Molly. No problem." Frank entered the living room, his woolen shirt untucked, tiny pieces of leaves stuck to it here and there.

"Frank, this is Jeffrey Jepson, my landlord's son. Mr. Jepson, this is Frank, my next-door neighbor."

The two men shook hands, and Jeffrey scowled at both Frank and Molly.

"How can I help you, Mr. Jepson?"

"I came to have a *private* conversation with you, Ms. Bates."

"Oh, there's nothing you can't say in front of Frank. Please, go ahead."

Jepson looked at Frank and then at Molly. His face pinched and his nose wrinkled. He squinted his eyes subtly, but she was watching closely for his reaction. Frank walked over and sat on the sofa, crossing his left ankle over his right knee. Molly was so grateful Frank had come when JT called him. She looked at Frank and smiled. "I guess my manners have escaped me. Can I get either of you something to drink? I still have coffee or water. I could make tea if you prefer."

"Nothing for me, Molly. I'm good, but maybe Mr. Jepson would like something?" Frank pointedly looked at Jepson.

"Ah, n-no. N-nothing for me."

Molly sat on the sofa next to Frank and pointed to a chair at a forty-five-degree angle for Jepson to sit down. "So, Mr. Jepson, what did you need to discuss?"

"I...well, I just wanted to discuss the purchase of this house. I...well... um." Jeffrey started patting his breast pocket down.

"Hi, Frank; sorry I'm late." Ryder strode in, looking entirely like the sexy, gorgeous man he is. She let out a long breath and relaxed her hands on her lap. Ryder quickly shook hands with Frank. He leaned down and kissed Molly on the lips, stood back a bit and winked at her. Then he turned his attention to Jepson.

"Mr. Jepson, I didn't realize we were expecting you today." Ryder reached over and firmly shook Jepson's hand.

Jepson's eyes glinted narrowly at Ryder. He cleared his throat as Ryder sat next to Molly and wrapped his arm around her shoulders. He gave her a little squeeze of reassurance and kissed the top of her head.

Jepson patted his jacket pocket and quickly stood. "I have to apologize; I thought I had the Offer to Purchase with me, but I seem to have forgotten it. I'll bring it by a little later."

Ryder quickly interjected, "Actually, Molly and I are meeting with our banker in a few hours to write up an Offer. Our banker will get it to you for signature, and I believe you'll need to sign it and return it to her." Ryder's voice was firm, and he never moved his eyes from Jepson's. His jaw tightened as he waited for Jepson to respond.

"Oh, right...right. I was wondering what was going on with it all. It's... It's been a couple of weeks, and I hadn't heard anything from you. I'll be going then. Sorry to have bothered you, it seems you have quite a lot going on." He scurried to the front door.

"There's usually someone here working with Molly or me. I have a very large family, so someone is usually hanging around. It was nice seeing you."

~

Jepson quickly walked out the door with Ryder on his heels. Frank and Molly both stood, but stayed where they were. Ryder stood at the door until Jepson got into his car and drove away. Once only his taillights were visible, he locked the storm door and the main door. He turned to Molly, and she ran to him and wrapped her arms tightly around him. He cupped her head and pressed her against his chest, the anger rising in his body at the way her body shook and her face displayed her fears. He looked over at Frank.

"Thanks so much for running over here so fast. I can't tell you how grateful we are."

Frank nodded. "To be honest with you, I thought it was just Molly being a little paranoid, but as soon as I saw the look on his face, I knew that wasn't the case." He glanced at the door. "That one isn't right."

Molly turned and smiled at Frank. "I'm never paranoid!"

Frank chuckled. Ryder cupped Molly's face in his hands. "Are you okay, babe?"

"Geez. I was scared shitless. He kept knocking and knocking and then when he yelled that he wanted to talk to me, it scared me. I was so happy to see Frank walk over. Thank you so much, Frank."

Frank nodded his graying head. "May I ask what the deal is with him?"

Molly took a deep breath. "Mr. Jepson—Ellison Jepson, my landlord —passed away a couple of weeks ago. Jeffrey is his son and found a sheet of paper in Mr. Jepson's safe to sell me the house." She glanced at Ryder and then to Frank. "The first time he came here to speak with me about it, he cornered me in the kitchen. He creeped me out, but luckily, Ryder came in before anything happened." She stepped toward the kitchen. "I'd like to ask Pattie, our banker, to put her contact information on the contract for Jeffrey to respond to her directly. I don't want to deal with him anymore."

Frank nodded. "I'll keep my eyes open from now on. I had no idea Ellison passed away. We haven't been in contact since he moved out and you moved in."

∽

The next evening, Ryder and Molly joined Tammy and Danny for wings at The Stadium Bar and then went to The Barn for drinks and dancing.

They found a table not far from the dance floor and Molly and Tammy headed out to dance while Ryder and Danny sat at the table drinking their beers. Ryder loved watching Molly dance. Her beautiful body was so graceful when she moved. Her full breasts, one of his favorite things about her body, moved when she moved. Tonight, she was wearing turquoise jeans with a soft gray sweater and tall gray heels that allowed her cute little toes to peek out. She had dangly turquoise earrings that wiggled and sparkled while she moved around.

As he watched her and Tammy move around the dance floor, he couldn't help but smile.

A feminine voice broke his perusal of the woman he loved. "What are you up to?"

Ryder swung his head toward the voice only to see Rachel standing at his table looking at him. He turned his gaze to Danny and then back to Rachel.

"What do you want now, Rachel?"

She laughed at his tone, slowly licked her lips and leaned on the table, exposing more of her cleavage.

"Aren't you going to introduce me to your friend?" She slid her gaze to Danny and smiled.

"Danny, this is Rachel. Rachel, Danny."

Danny nodded at her and looked back at Ryder, understanding flowing between them.

"Do you want to dance with me, Ryder?" Rachel giggled.

He took a deep breath and let it out slowly. "No, Rachel, I don't want to dance with you. If I wanted to dance, I would dance with Molly, not you. You know I'm with her, so why do you insist on constantly trying to start shit every time you see us here?"

"Come on, Ryder," she whined. "We had fun together. I just want to have more fun; that's all."

"We had sex a couple of times—that's it. It was never anything more, and it never will be. Try and get that through your head."

"Well, you keep coming back here, knowing I'll be here."

Ryder shook his head and looked at Danny again. He chanced a look at the dance floor to see Molly watching, her eyebrows raised in question. Shit!

"We come here because Kevin, the owner, is a very good friend of my dad. It's a bar my whole family comes to, and I'm not going to avoid going to a place my family frequents because of you. There's no reason we can't both be here without this constant bullshit. I'm with Molly. I love Molly. End of story."

"But..."

"What's going on here?" Ryder looked up to see JT standing at the table and Gunnar on his way over.

"Same old shit, man," Ryder responded as JT and Danny shook hands.

Gunnar arrived at the table and shoved himself between Ryder and Rachel, then waved at Molly and Tammy on the dance floor. Molly waved back and smirked as Rachel scowled, first at Gunnar, then Molly. Tammy started laughing, returned Gunnar's wave, then turned back to Molly to finish dancing out the remainder of the song. Rachel stalked back to her table as Molly and Tammy came back to join the men.

"Hey there, how are you?" Molly greeted Gunnar with a hug and whispered in his ear, "Thanks for helping with Rachel."

Gunnar smiled at her and whispered back, "I hate that bitch, and I'm sick of her bullshit."

When he pulled away, he winked at her. Molly said hello to JT while Tammy greeted everyone in turn.

"You know, it's so weird looking at the two of you standing next to each other. Who would have thought something this strange would happen to people I know," Tammy said between sips of her drink.

Gunnar laughed and looked at Molly. "Yeah. All my life I wanted a sibling. I'm glad I have her now, but I wish she would have been around a long time ago." He nudged Molly with his shoulder, and she nodded in agreement.

"There were so many times in my life I could have used having an older brother. You have no idea some of the things I had to endure!" Molly said.

Tammy gasped then froze; she didn't think Molly had told anyone about her stepfather. The drinks must be making her tongue loose. All four men stared at the expression on Tammy's face, clearly confused by what she meant. Tammy glared at Molly, and Molly realized she must have said more than what she had intended.

Gunnar cocked his head to the side as he turned to look at Molly. "Like when?"

It was Molly's turn to freeze up. *Shit!* She shouldn't have had that fourth drink; she knows better than that. Trying to gather her thoughts as quickly as she could, she looked at Tammy, horror written on her face.

"You know high school boys can be evil," Tammy offered.

Molly looked relieved as she slid her gaze to Tammy and then back to the table.

"Hey. Something happen to you as a kid, Molly? You can tell me, you know."

Molly looked up at Gunnar and shook her head. Gunnar leaned down and kissed the top of Molly's head and looked at Ryder. Ryder's brows drew together as he flexed his hands and rolled his shoulders.

# 17

## ELLISON

Some days were just made for puttering around the house. That was today. Ryder was working out with his brothers at their house, and Molly was organizing her office space. She had neglected it a little over the past few days.

On her knees in front of her desk, she pulled open the bottom drawer and began filing invoices from this month. Hearing a thump at the back of the house, she froze. Nothing. Her imagination was getting the best of her lately. She continued filing as her phone rang.

Reaching forward to grab it off the desk, she quickly swiped the answer icon, "Memories by Molly."

"You'll be happy to know I'm out. I'll be around to collect what's mine."

Acid filled her stomach, and her heart stammered out a rapid beat. "How...when did you get out?" She tried swallowing the knot of cotton in her throat.

All she heard was laughing on the other end of the phone and then the line went dead.

She sat back on her heels as her heart thumped so loudly she couldn't hear the music coming from the stereo. The trembling in her hands and tightness in her neck threatened to reduce her to tears. She would not let this bastard *ever* touch her again. In spite of the fact she thought she was damaged, she'd found happiness with Ryder.

Taking deep, calming breaths, she pulled her phone up and swiped her finger along her contacts until she came to the one person with whom she could freely talk. Tapping the smiling picture staring at her, Molly lifted the phone to her ear.

"Hey, there girl, what's happening?"

At the sound of Tammy's voice, Molly's composure crumbled.

"Tammy," she sobbed into the phone. Trying to form words, she spoke again, "He's out."

"What...who's... Fuck! When?"

Swallowing again and rubbing the back of her neck, she whispered, "He just called me."

"No. How did he get your number?"

"He called a few weeks ago. Told me he got my number from the Rolling Thunder video." Molly's voice cracked. "Tammy. He said he's coming to collect what's his." She hiccupped and swiped at the tears rolling down her cheeks.

Tammy's soft voice questioned, "What did Ryder say?"

"I haven't told him yet. Things are so good; how could I tell him? He'll think I'm dirty."

Tammy took a deep breath. Softening her voice, she said, "No, he won't, Molly. Just like I don't, he won't either. You have to tell him."

# 18

# CHRISTMAS TREE

"Tammy just called, and she and Danny are going to get a Christmas tree at the tree farm by Danny's house. They wanted to know if we wanted to pick our tree up at the same time. Are you interested?"

"That sounds like fun. We haven't even talked about that. What kind of a tree do you like to get, Molly?"

She wrinkled her face as she took a deep breath and looked at Ryder. "I usually don't get a tree. This will be the first year since...I guess since I was eleven."

Ryder's brows pinched together. "Why didn't you get a tree?"

She looked past Ryder at the kitchen light. Then she looked out the window for a little while.

"Hey. You with me here?"

"Yeah. Um, well, since my parents divorced, we just didn't get a tree anymore." Molly's eyes watered with unshed tears. Ryder stepped forward and wrapped his arms around her.

"Oh, babe. I'm sorry. Do you want to talk about it?"

Molly shook her head vigorously. "No. Not really."

"Okay, well I say two things. First, let's get us a Christmas tree to celebrate our first Christmas together. And second, there's something going on, and I want to know. For the past week, you've been edgy and withdrawn. Have I done something?"

"No, of course not. I know I owe you an explanation, Ryder; I just can't yet."

He wrapped his arms around her and held her close. "I won't lie to you; it's been killing me watching you. Mom says it will help you to talk about it and get it off your chest."

She nodded. "It might." Taking a deep breath, she continued. "Maybe we can just come back here for pizza after we play lumberjacks."

"Sounds good, baby."

He watched Molly call Tammy. Each day he grew more in love with her. This past week she'd changed. She was nervous at little sounds, and she was constantly looking out the window. It just broke his heart to find out she didn't have Christmas trees growing up. He couldn't imagine not having a tree and presents and a big, loud family around. Of course, their Christmases were about to get bigger. This year, Joci, Gunnar, and Molly are added to their family, and next year he would have another little sister or brother to play with.

What on earth happened when her parents divorced? She was awful tight-lipped about it all. He could ask Tammy what was going on, but he really wanted Molly to tell him herself.

She broke into his thoughts. "Okay. We should meet them at Danny's house in about an hour and then we'll all come back here. Should we stop at Papa Murphy's and pick up a fresh pizza?"

"Sounds fantastic."

◞

Tammy squealed. "This is going to be so much fun. We're putting our tree in the living room, in the front window. Where are you guys putting your tree?"

Molly looked at Tammy and smiled. "Our tree?"

Tammy squealed. "I'm moving in with Danny this week! Isn't that exciting?"

Molly hugged Tammy and then Danny. "Very exciting. Things seem to be going great for you guys."

"They are." Tammy smiled brightly at Danny as he wrapped his arm around her shoulders. "Things are changing so fast in our lives. Even Cara has a boyfriend now. We should get together soon and go out for a girl's night."

Molly's smile didn't reach her eyes. "Sure. Sounds fun."

They climbed in their vehicles and drove a couple of miles to the tree farm. Once there, they began their trek through the woods in search of the perfect trees.

Ryder pointed to a tall pine, narrow and sparse. "I like this one."

Molly shook her head. "It's too scrawny."

Tammy found one she liked, but it was about nine feet tall. Danny told her it wouldn't fit. They began to argue about it, so Ryder and Molly headed in a different direction to give them privacy to work it out. After wandering around the trees for a while, Molly spotted one, and her face lit up.

"This one is perfect. It still has pine cones in it, and we can decorate it in a rustic theme." She clapped her hands as she hopped up and down with glee. It was the first time in a week he saw that spark again; there was no way he was taking this joy from her. He watched her eyes light up and her smile spread across her whole face, and he couldn't help but pull her into his arms and kiss her.

"Jesus, you're a beautiful woman. You take my breath away, Molly."

She wrapped her arms around his neck and kissed him back. "I feel the same way about you, Ryder. You are a good-looking man."

They kissed until they were breathless. "I guess I better cut this tree down before we get so hot we melt the snow," he husked out.

She burst out laughing. "Good idea."

Ryder worked at cutting down the tree. It wasn't a huge tree, so it didn't take very long, and with his muscles, it really wasn't that hard to do. They started dragging it toward the spot where they left Danny and Tammy and found them lying in the snow making out next to a tree they had just cut down.

"I guess we weren't the only ones melting snow." Molly giggled.

Tammy laughed and so did Danny. They stood and started pulling their trees toward their trucks. Ryder had learned a while back not to ask Danny if he needed help. It pissed him off. He would try and do everything himself first, and if he struggled too much, then he would ask for help. But Ryder started ahead of Danny and Tammy, dragging their tree to knock the snow down a little. They chatted and talked the whole way back.

"This pizza is good. I've never had this kind before. What did you call it?"

"It's Ryder's favorite. It's called Mama's Special."

They sat in the living room of Ryder and Molly's place, eating pizza, drinking beer, and watching television.

"So, did your landlord sign the Offer to Purchase yet?"

"Ugh, wait till I tell you what happened." Molly gasped.

She proceeded to tell Danny and Tammy about the episode with Jepson. Tammy was horrified, and Danny looked pissed. He looked at Ryder. "What happens next?"

"I called my uncle Tommy; he's a cop. Not a lot we can do, but I gave him a description of his vehicle, and they have officers driving by a couple of times each shift to make sure his car isn't in the area. He didn't sign the Offer to Purchase yet, but he has another day before the Offer expires."

"Gawd, that's frustrating. Sorry, Moll."

Molly shrugged. "Nothing we can do but wait."

They continued eating their pizza as Danny and Tammy talked about moving in together and the Christmas decorations they had purchased for the house. Danny loved the addition added to his home and told everyone how much easier it had made his life already.

They left around eight-thirty to decorate their tree.

Molly was excited to decorate theirs. "I have some older decorations in the basement from my mom's house. I haven't looked at them in years, but maybe some of them are still usable."

"I can go down and pull the boxes out for you. Where are they?"

"I need to go down and look. It's been years, and I'm not sure how much stuff I'm going to need to move to get to them. Can we do it tomorrow?"

"Well, tomorrow we can go and buy new ornaments for our tree. If you find some in the basement you'd like to keep, you can just add them to the tree." He looked at the tree and then into her eyes. His voice grew husky. "But, for right now, Molly, I want you to stand in front of that tree and strip for me. You will be the only ornament in front of the tree, and I can't think of anything more beautiful than that."

She smiled and slowly stood up. Slowly stepping to the tree, she turned and stood between it and Ryder and button by button, began undressing.

As she popped the last button on her blouse she let the soft silky fabric slide from her shoulders and fall to the floor at her feet in a puddle. He raised his brows and licked his lips, and she slowly slid the zipper on her jeans to the bottom. Shimmying her hips side to side, she slowly ran her tongue along her lips and watched as Ryder rubbed his thickening cock through his jeans.

She lightly kicked her jeans away and reached behind to unsnap her bra. As soon as the clasp released, her full breasts fell from the lacy fabric, and she caught them in her hands. She fingered her nipples, creating little peaks and Ryder unzipped his jeans to relieve the pressure. She was beautiful, this woman of his. He couldn't imagine life without her in it. He was going to marry this girl. They were going to have beautiful babies one day. But he wanted her to himself for a few years first.

Pulling her bottom lip between her teeth, she shimmied out of her panties and let them fall to the floor. She gave them a little toss with her toes toward Ryder and stood before him, naked and waiting.

He smiled and slowly rose from the sofa to stand before her. He held her head in his hands and kissed her slowly. He explored her mouth, tasted her lips, and kissed his way around her whole face. He slowly dropped to his knees before her, sliding his hands down her waist. He lifted his face and sucked a nipple into his mouth, gently loving her breast with his tongue and his lips.

Her hands cupped Ryder's head as he loved each breast in turn and began kissing his way down her body. He licked and kissed her torso and her hips. Very slowly, he swiped his tongue across her clit. He heard her whimper, and he smiled against her. He parted her moist folds with deft fingers and touched her clit again, this time, making contact so profound, her knees shook.

"Hold on to my shoulders if you need to, babe," he rasped.

She did just that.

"Open your legs for me, Molly. Give me access to that beautiful pussy of yours."

Slowly, he slid two fingers inside of her—in and out-- as he continued licking and sucking at her body. She whimpered. Her legs shook, her body was flushed and warm, and a fine sheen of sweat had formed on her forehead, chest, and face. He applied more pressure to her clit and crooked his fingers inside of her, causing an orgasm to burst from her body with fury. She cried out as her weakened legs gave out beneath her.

He caught her and laid her on the floor next to him. He raised himself above her and slid his jeans down his hips, he rolled her over onto her belly and pulled her back until her knees were up to her chest.

"We didn't get to this yesterday; tonight, I'm going to come in here." He rubbed Molly's tight, puckered anal opening with his fingers. He added a little pressure, and she stiffened, waiting for him to enter her.

"Stay right here, just like this. Move your hands and arms above your head, palms flat on the floor. I'll be right back."

She did as she was told. Her breathing was raspy and ragged. He came back into the room, and she turned her head to see him. She huffed out a breath when she saw him standing naked before her.

He kneeled down behind her and ran his hands over the globes of her ass, gently kneading and enjoying the feel of her soft skin against his. He squeezed the lubricant into his hand and warmed it between his palms.

He gently applied lube to the outside of Molly's puckered opening and gently pushed a finger into her. She gasped as his finger slid in. "Breathe, baby. Take a deep breath and let it out slowly."

He pulled his finger out and pushed back in slowly, allowing her body to get used to the feel. Gently, he inserted a second finger, opening her up more for him. All the while, he crooned sweet words of praise in her ear—how beautiful she was, how special she was, how much he loved her and wanted her always.

Her body felt good, his invasion of her behind was the most sensual act he could think of, forbidden in some ways, primal in others.

He whispered in her ear, "I'm coming in, babe. Are you ready?"

"Yes," she breathed out.

He seated the broad head of his cock at her opening, applying a small amount of pressure. "When I push in, I need you to gently push out to ease my way."

Her voice shaky, she said, "Okay."

He slowly pushed into her, allowing her time to adjust. He shook from restraint and excitement. Molly's opening gave way and allowed him entrance. He slid in a few inches, and they both gasped. Still allowing more time to adjust, he reached around and rubbed her clit, sending new sensations throughout her body. He heard her gasp and felt her push herself back into him, and he slid in a little more, hissing out a breath as he did.

Her voice shook. "Please, Ryder. Take me. Please."

He groaned and began moving, pulling himself out to the head and pushing back in. Out and back in, over and over, slowly, allowing each of them the pleasure of feeling him slide in and out.

"Jesus. So fucking tight...so fucking amazing. Your little ass is squeezing the cum right out of me, Molly." He groaned.

She whimpered at his words. "Ryder..." Her voice was barely a whisper.

He wanted to show her with his body what he felt his words just couldn't say. He didn't feel shy around her anymore; quite the opposite. She made him feel bold, strong, and so in control of himself. It had only been a few months, but she made him feel like the man he wanted to be.

"I love you, Molly. I love you with my heart, my soul, and my body."

"Ryder. God, Ryder, I love you. So much, I'm afraid."

He nodded slightly as she whimpered. Silently they communicated their readiness and need to come together to complete this moment that neither would ever forget.

# 19

## BREAKING UP

Molly's cell phone rang and she stood to grab it from the counter. She didn't recognize the number on the screen but answered anyway in her professional voice. "Memories by Molly, how may I help you?"

She walked to her office where she kept her calendar in case an appointment needed to be made. The voice on the other end of the line froze her in her tracks. The voice she dreaded. The voice that invaded her nightmares.

"Are you ready for me?"

Her head spun, the color around her faded to gray, and she was having trouble breathing.

"I'm not interested in seeing you."

She sat at her desk, holding the phone to her ear with a shaking hand, struggling to continue holding it. She closed her eyes as she willed herself to calm down and think.

"You're not that hard to find. Now that I'm out of jail I'm going to pay a visit to that slut of a mother of yours."

Fear and anger welled up. "Leave her alone. She doesn't even know where she is or who she's talking to most of the time."

"Well, well, well. Guess what, bitch? You don't get to tell me what to do and when to do it. I'll visit who I want and when I want. I served my time; there's no restraining order."

She sucked in a couple of shaky breaths. This couldn't be happening. Why? Why was he out of jail?

His disgusting voice broke into her scrambled thoughts. "I watched you last night. You stripped naked for some horny fucking man. You're mine, Molly, do you understand me? I'll kill that fucker if I see you with him again, got it?"

"You leave him alone. He's done nothing wrong, and neither have I." She closed her eyes and willed her breathing to slow. The bile in her stomach churned.

"Your whole life is wrong, you little bitch. I told you that first time, the least you could do was spread your legs for me since I was the one duped by your slut of a mother. She had me raise you as my own for nine fucking years. I paid for your clothes, your food, a roof over your head. Your pussy is mine, Molly. Get rid of that fucking bastard you've been letting sample what's mine or I will kill him. The other one, too."

Her eyes flew open. "What are you talking about? There is no other one."

"I saw him there, too. Walking out of the backyard the other day. You're a busy little slut. Get rid of both of them, or you'll find out what I'll be willing to do. I'll be watching. You have until this evening to get rid of them. Disobey me and find out what I'll do to them and your crazy fucking mother."

She pulled the phone from her ear and hit the end call button. She was numb and didn't know what he was talking about when he said there was someone other than Ryder. He was a crazy bastard. But she had no doubt that given the chance, Lancaster Elson would kill Ryder, or at the very least, hurt him badly. He was a vicious bastard, sneaky and conniving. She needed to break it off with Ryder so Lancaster would leave him alone. If he saw that she wasn't with him anymore, he'd be safe. The biggest problem was going to be living without her heart. Ryder was her heart and her soul, the very breath she depended on to live. How would she get through each day without him in her life?

She sat for what felt like hours trying to figure out another way. That was the problem; she couldn't see one. He was right; there wasn't a restraining order against him and how could she even get one? He hadn't done anything wrong...yet. She'd never pressed charges against him when she was a girl.

She stood and walked to the bedroom to start packing Ryder's things into boxes. Good thing he hadn't actually moved in yet. When he came over tonight, she would tell him they were over. She had to. She had no doubt that Lancaster would hurt him. She'd always known that her past would tear them apart, but she was drawn in by Ryder. She'd been powerless to stop the pull he had on her. She had no idea how she would make herself tell him they were over, but she had to have the strength.

~

"Hey, what's with all the boxes?"

Ryder walked into the kitchen from the garage and saw the boxes piled on the steps by the door. Maybe Molly had pulled the boxes of Christmas stuff out of the basement. He told her he would take care of it. Silly woman. He looked around the room and didn't see her anywhere.

"Moll?"

He walked into the living room, still no Molly. He continued his way through the house and didn't see her anywhere. Walking back into the kitchen, he saw a note on the counter. The dread in his stomach started rising to the surface. He picked up the note and unfolded it.

*Ryder, I regret to tell you this, but it just isn't working out between us. If I look at the signs, it's all there. Jepson didn't sign the Offer, which means we weren't meant to have this house. You put off moving in with me because of Gunnar and me, seems to be another sign. I've been feeling this way for a while now and decided to go ahead and make a break. Please take your things and leave. I have them all packed and in boxes on the steps in the garage. I will be with friends tonight. Please don't make this difficult, it's for the best. Molly.*

What the fuck? Ryder's head spun. Break up? No way in hell was she breaking up with him! Signs? Bullshit! Last night was the best night ever in his life, his beautiful woman under their first Christmas tree. No way she'd been feeling bad about their relationship. He reeled, couldn't breathe and his heart beat so fast he thought it would grow legs and leave his body. He grabbed the counter to steady himself.

*Think Ryder, think. What the fuck happened between last night and today?*

Nothing. He couldn't come up with a thing. Bullshit! She wasn't breaking up with him—not without explanation, and certainly not by leaving him a fucking note!

He got in his truck and left. He didn't know where he was going, just driving without direction. An hour later, he found himself at Danny and Tammy's. He knocked on their door, and Danny opened the door to a disheveled and sad sight.

"Holy fuck! What's going on with you?"

Ryder's voice was barely a whisper. "Have you seen Molly? Is she here?"

Danny stepped aside and motioned for Ryder to come in. He looked to Tammy where she sat on the sofa with her legs curled up under her body. Her brows furrowed when she looked at Ryder.

"What's happened? Is Molly okay? What's going on?"

Ryder dejectedly looked at Tammy; he'd hoped she was here. He shook his head and tears sprang to his eyes. "Have you seen her?"

Tammy jumped up and walked to Ryder. "No. I haven't seen her all day. What happened?"

She led Ryder to the sofa and both she and Danny sat on either side of him. Ryder swallowed a few times to get himself under control. "She broke up with me. In a fucking note!" His voice cracked. He scraped his hands through his spiky hair and then down his face, trying to wipe away the worry and pain.

"What? She loves you. She's told me so many times that she never dreamed she could be so happy. She wouldn't break up with you. Certainly, not in a note."

Ryder bent his head and grabbed both sides of it between his hands and rested his elbows on his knees. Tammy didn't even know where Molly was? Tammy knew everything about Molly. Why wouldn't Molly tell her about this? It made no sense at all.

"I came home today, my stuff was packed into boxes, and there was a note on the counter telling me to take my stuff and leave. She said she was looking at the signs, and they told her that it wasn't working out between us. Her car is still at home, but she isn't there."

"What? That's such bullshit! I'm calling her."

Tammy grabbed her phone and hit Molly's number and waited for her to answer. Her phone rang and rang, but Molly didn't pick up. "What the fuck? She's not going to answer MY call?"

When Molly's voicemail picked up, Tammy left her a message. "Molly, what the fuck is going on? Call me right away when you get this."

Danny's voice was soft, but clear. "Where would she be, Tammy? Can you think of any place she might go?"

Tammy sat for a moment, thinking. Molly always came to her. Tammy knew everything about Molly's awful life. From her parentage to her stepfather's abuse—all of it. Why wouldn't Molly come to her with something like this?

"She always comes to me. I can't imagine where she is or what she's up to. Seriously, this is the weirdest thing."

"Would she go and see her mom?"

"No. Her mom doesn't even know who Molly is. On her best days, Tori calls Molly, Nancy. On her worst days, she just stares at Molly and doesn't really say anything at all. No, I don't think she'd go to see her mom."

# 20

## LANCASTER ELSON

Molly had been sitting in this fucking hotel room for two damn days, and she hadn't showered or washed her hair at all. She didn't want to breathe, but she had no idea how to stop doing that. She'd spent most of her time lying in bed and had gone out only once for food and bottled water. She tried to make sense of all this and to come up with a way to change it. So far, she hadn't come up with anything.

A knock on the door pulled her out of her sadness. She walked to the door, wiping her hands down her jeans, thinking the maid had come to clean.

"I don't need maid service," she said through the door.

"Towels, Miss."

Blowing out a breath, Molly cracked the door open. She screamed just as Lancaster Elson pushed his way into the room and closed the door behind him. He was gross looking, and he smelled bad like he hadn't showered in days. The stale stench of cigarette smoke clung to him. His clothes were ratty and torn, and his greasy hair was matted to his head. His teeth were crooked and yellow. How could she have ever felt anything for this man? She'd thought of him as her father for so many years. Now all she saw was an abuser, rapist, and thug.

"Well. What do you have to say for yourself?"

She shook her head slightly to make her head catch up to this horrific turn of events. "I don't understand what you mean."

"I mean, you little slut, that right in your living room, in front of the tree, you let some son-of-a-bitch touch you. Fuck you. What do you have to say for yourself?"

"Nothing." Molly's voice was small and weak. She knew he wanted her to argue with him so he could hit her. He probably would anyway. It didn't matter anymore. If she didn't have Ryder, she didn't want to live anyway.

"Nothing? You stupid little cunt! Nothing? Did you think because I was in jail that you could run around fucking anything with a cock? I was the first one in that pussy, you bitch, and I'll be the last one in it. Do you understand me?"

Lancaster raised his hand and slapped her, hard, across the face. Molly reeled back a few steps, her hand holding her face where he had connected. Nausea rolled through her body. She leaned forward and threw up on the floor at Lancaster's feet. The thought of him ever touching her again was simply the most disgusting thing she could think of.

Lancaster laughed at her. "Do I disgust you? Tough shit, get over it."

She wiped at her mouth and wiped her hands on her jeans. She didn't know what to do. She couldn't let him touch her again. She just couldn't.

Her voice shook. "How did you find me?"

"I'll always find you. Lucky for me, I learned how to find people. I followed you here and watched to make sure that fucker didn't come. It took me a day to find out which room you were in. Good thing I'm patient. Just for good measure, I visited your mother. Fucking crazy bitch, that one."

Molly sucked in a breath. Good God, he was with her mother? She was horrified.

Her body heated with anger, tears threatened, but she refused to let them fall. "I asked you to leave her alone. I've done what you wanted and broke up with Ryder. Why did you bother her?"

"I didn't fucking bother her. She doesn't even know what fucking day it is. What about the other bastard that you've been fucking?"

"There isn't anyone else. I don't know what you mean."

Lancaster smirked. "That fat bastard that's been hanging around the house. He's been there almost every day. Don't play stupid with me, Molly."

She shook her head. There hadn't been anyone else at the house besides Ryder. Lancaster must really be cracking up. Now she was in this room alone with him, and there was no way she was going to let him touch her again. No way!

She took a step back. Lancaster followed. Molly froze, not wanting him to follow her and get any closer. "I need to use the bathroom. Brush my teeth."

Lancaster nodded his head toward the bathroom. "Don't close the door. I'll break it down if you do."

She closed her eyes. She needed to calm down and think. She needed to get out of here. Maybe if she just explained everything to Ryder, he could think of some way for them to get out of this. His uncle is a cop, so maybe his uncle could keep him safe while they figured out how to stop Lancaster from doing anything to Ryder. Shit! To think she'd handled this all wrong was an understatement. She should have been straight with Ryder from the beginning. He probably didn't want to have anything to do with her now.

Slowly, she walked to the bathroom and pulled her toothbrush and toothpaste from her toiletry bag. She turned the water on and began brushing her teeth. She peeked out the door, and Lancaster had made himself comfortable on her bed. Controlling her urge to vomit again, she slowly reached into her back pocket and pulled her cell phone out. She hadn't turned it on in a while, but she did now. Hopefully, she'd get a chance to call 911, telling them Lancaster was holding her against her will. Once she had him arrested, she would be able to get a restraining order against him, but she had to get out of here first.

She finished brushing her teeth and methodically put her toiletries in the bag. She slipped her phone into her pocket as she walked from the bathroom toward the door.

"Where do you think you're going?"

"Out. I don't have any food in here, and I need some aspirin. I have a headache."

"You're not going anywhere. Sit your ass down, now!"

"Are you holding me hostage?" She stood straight, her spine rigid. She couldn't be timid with him anymore.

"Don't you think you have the upper hand with me, Molly. You try and walk out of this room, I'm paying that boyfriend of yours a visit at work. Rolling Thunder, right?"

Shit! She hoped she could call Ryder and warn him about Lancaster right away, but what if he wouldn't take her calls? He probably didn't ever want to see her again. If she couldn't get to him before Lancaster, he could be hurt, maybe killed.

"Why would you risk going to jail again by trying to hurt Ryder?"

"Because he has been tasting what's mine. No man does that."

"I'm not yours. I never have been." Her jaw tightened, her body heated higher than an oven.

"Oh, yes you are, Molly. You are mine." A sickening grin slid across his face as he sat up on the bed.

"No, I'm not. You raped me when I was eleven years old. Rape. That doesn't make me yours. That makes you a rapist! And you will not do it again. Never again will you touch me."

She bolted to the door and flung it open. She burst into the hallway, almost running into the maid service cart. She ran past the cart, giving it a little pull behind her, in case Lancaster decided to follow her. She ran down the flight of stairs and out to the parking lot to her rental car.

$\sim$

Ryder sat at the table, surrounded by his family—Joci, Jeremiah, Gunnar, JT, his Uncle Tommy, even Tammy and Danny were there. They were at Molly's house, trying to figure out how to find her. Ryder had looked everywhere. They'd been calling her phone to no avail. Tommy had traced her credit card and found no activity. Nothing.

"Do you believe him, Uncle Tommy? Do you believe that son-of-a-bitch, Jepson?"

"Yeah, I do. We've questioned him over and over. He was stalking her, and he'd recorded the two of you having sex. He got off on that. He stole her panties and some of her pictures, but I don't think he has her. If he did, he wouldn't have come back here in the first place to sit and listen. He would be with her. Plus, we saw the rental car company come here and give Molly keys to the rental in one of the trail cams Jepson had installed."

Fuck! Ryder's mind reeled. Right after Molly took off, his Uncle Tommy and another off-duty officer had gone through the house looking for clues that might lead them to where Molly might have gone. They'd found Jeffrey Jepson, sitting in the basement, surrounded by boxes and Molly's things. He'd installed a microphone and pushed it up through the vent and into the bedroom. While he listened to them have sex, he would masturbate as he fondled the panties he'd stolen from Molly's dresser drawer. It was creepy knowing he'd been in the house, listening to them, for God only knows how long.

Jepson said it had only been since he first met Molly. He had keys to the house because his dad was Molly's landlord. He let himself in the first time and then opened the window in the basement that led to the backyard. He would shimmy through each day to let himself in the house. He set up a little area in the back of the basement below the bedroom, which is where he would sit and masturbate.

They found trail cameras installed in the trees around the house so Jepson could take pictures of them coming and going. Once he'd figured out their pattern, he would let himself in and wait for them to come home. What a sick fuck!

"I have an idea," Tammy said, looking at Gunnar.

"Molly told me you look like your father. Her mom called you Keith when she saw you. Maybe you could go with us and see if Tori has seen Molly or would tell you something that would give us an idea of where she might be. I know it's a long shot, but if Molly went there to say good-bye or something, maybe it would trigger Tori's memory."

Everyone turned and looked at Gunnar. He dipped his head in acknowledgment but remained quiet for some time.

"Here's what I think." He rubbed his forehead with his fingers as if he could wipe away the worry. "Something has happened to her. To spook her. This isn't her normal behavior; we all see it."

He looked around the room and each person acknowledged his comments with a nod or glance.

That being said, "I'll do anything to find her. Let's give it a try."

Ryder ran his hands through his hair for the thousandth time today. What the hell happened to her? His emotions were all over the place. First, his heart was broken, and then he feared something terrible had happened to her. His emotions bounced back and forth like a ping pong ball. If she *was* dumping him, she owed him an explanation. She owed Tammy an explanation too. Hell, she owed everyone an explanation.

They each stood to go to the nursing home when Tammy's phone rang. She pulled it from her pocket and looked at the screen.

"It's Molly. Oh, thank God." She tapped the icon to answer. Everyone stood completely still, waiting to hear the conversation.

"Put it on speaker," Ryder said anxiously.

With more bite than she meant, she snapped, "Molly—thank God you called! Where the *hell* are you?"

Molly's voice broke; it bounced as she ran. "Tammy. I need help. He's after Ryder and me. He said he's going to kill him. I was going to call Ryder and warn him, but I was afraid he wouldn't take my call. You need to warn him that he's in danger."

Tammy's eyes rounded as she stared at the phone like it was a lifeline. "Molly. Who? Who's after you and where are you?"

They all listened. She was out of breath, and she sounded scared.

"Lancaster. Lancaster's after me. He said if I didn't break up with Ryder he would kill him. He found me today and..." Her voice cracked as a sob escaped.

"I couldn't let him touch me again, Tam. I just couldn't. He's chasing me now. Please warn Ryder."

"Molly!" Ryder barked. "Where are you? Tommy's here, he'll send the police."

They heard a car door slam; then they heard a loud bang and glass breaking. Molly screamed and dropped her phone. They could hear someone yelling in the distance.

"You fucking little cunt. Get your ass out of that car."

Tommy turned into the living room and immediately called the station asking for a trace on Molly's phone and that officers be immediately dispatched to her location.

They heard another crash and Molly screamed. Then the engine of her vehicle revved up. They could hear tires squealing and the sound of her phone bouncing around the floor of the car. Ryder's stomach rolled. It was painful to hear Molly cry; she was in danger and needed help. He felt helpless as a newborn. Tommy returned to the kitchen and nodded at Ryder.

Molly yelled toward her phone. "I think I got away. I don't know if he has a car or what it looks like. I don't know where to go."

Ryder yelled at the phone, hoping she could hear him. "Molly. Come home. We're all here; you'll be safe. Come home."

Molly heard Ryder and glanced at her phone on the floor then back to the road as she navigated a corner, faster than she should. Her phone slid toward the hump in the floor, and she reached down to grab it but couldn't reach. A horn blaring captured her attention, and she righted her car, which had inched over in the other lane.

Ryder leaned closer to the phone and yelled, "Molly! Tell me you heard me. Come home!"

She began crying so hard, it was difficult to talk. She opened her mouth, and nothing came out. She swallowed and tried again. "I heard you. I'm coming home."

Tammy ran to the window in the living room, waiting to see Molly's car. It felt like hours. After about ten minutes, they could hear sirens through the phone. The police must have found her through the trace.

Tommy leaned forward and yelled into the phone. "Molly, this is Tommy Sheppard. We hear sirens. If they're behind you, pull over. I have them tracking your phone. They're there to help you. Can you hear me?"

"Yes," Molly yelled. It was all she could get out. She looked around her; she didn't see any police cars. She looked in her rearview mirror and saw nothing. But she could hear the sirens too. "Where are they? I can't see them." She wiped at her eyes with her hands, to clear her vision.

She passed a side street, then saw the police cars coming up to the intersection.

"I see them. I see them," Molly yelled.

She waited to see if they followed her. She didn't want to stop without protection in case Lancaster was behind her. She was using every ounce of reasoning power she had left to try and not freak out. Two police cars pulled in behind her, and she put her blinker on, letting them know she was pulling over. Braking, then putting the car in park, Molly used both hands to wipe the tears from her eyes. She turned her head to see the first officer slowly approaching the car from behind. He raised his gun and yelled at her, "Get out of the car, hands up, move slowly."

She gasped and stifled a sob. She opened the car door, which proved difficult, her hands shook so damn bad. When she was able to get the door open, she slowly moved her legs to the outside and put her hands up in the air. She never took her eyes from the officers. Standing up was going to be hard, her legs quivered and shook like crazy. Sobbing, she looked at the officer for help.

"Are you alone, Ms. Bates?"

Molly nodded her head; she couldn't speak at all.

"What happened to your windows?"

When she was able to catch her breath, she stammered, "H-he b-broke them."

"Who broke them and where is he?"

"L-Lancaster Elson...I d-don't know."

The officer was joined by the others to inspect the vehicle to ensure there was no one other than Molly. When the all clear was given, the first officer holstered his weapon and came to Molly's aid.

"I'm Officer Scott. I'll help you, Ms. Bates. Are you injured?"

Ryder let out a huge breath. They'd found her, thank God. His knees were weak, and he hit the chair behind him with a thud. He looked up at his dad, who quickly walked around the table and hugged him.

"They've got her. It'll be okay now, son."

Joci kneeled in front of Ryder and hugged him around the waist. She softly cried into his shirt. Jeremiah reached down and lifted Joci to her feet.

"You need to rest, baby. Come sit on the sofa with me while we wait for the police to bring Molly home."

Joci looked at Ryder. He nodded, and she allowed herself to be pulled into the living room to wait. Gunnar and JT sat next to Ryder at the table, not saying anything, just silently supporting him. They were good brothers. Tammy and Danny sat in the living room; Tammy watched out the window like a scout. The phone connection was still live, but they really couldn't hear anything more. The police must have put Molly in their car.

Ryder's mind reeled. Was she protecting him? Did she want to break up with him? Had she been hurt? Where has she been? He had so many questions he wanted to ask. Mostly, right now, he wanted to know that she was okay. How long would it take for them to get here with her?

He glanced down the hallway where Tommy was on the phone with the station. Hopefully, he'd have more information for them.

Ryder stood and wearily walked into the living room. He sat in an arm chair at a forty-five-degree angle to Tammy. He leaned forward, his forearms resting on his knees, his hands folded together. He looked into Tammy's eyes.

"I can piece together most of it, but tell me what Lancaster did to her. I'll ask her to tell me herself, but if I know, I can make sure I don't say anything wrong."

Danny put his arm around Tammy and kissed the side of her head. "You need to tell him, babe."

Her mouth formed a slight frown as her gaze never left his. Tammy took a deep breath and began to tell her story. "When Molly was nine, she had appendicitis and needed surgery. I think she told you this. Lancaster found out he wasn't her father when they needed to give her blood. Tori had lied to him and told him Molly was his. He was pissed, hurt, angry—all of it." She glanced at Joci then Danny. He nodded for her to continue. "He started verbally abusing Molly at first—calling her names, telling her she was stupid, clumsy, ignorant, and worthless. She had a hard time with it. She used to come to my house and cry and cry. She couldn't understand it. Then, Lancaster started drinking. When Molly was eleven, she came home from school one day, and Lancaster was there—already drunk."

Tammy wiped at tears that involuntarily slid down her cheeks. "Molly ran to her bedroom to stay away from him, but he barged in and forced himself on her. He told her she was his and she owed it to him to let him have sex with her as payment for all the years he'd raised her and put a roof over her head. He told her it was the least she could do."

"Jesus. That fucking bastard!" Ryder pounded his fist on the coffee table.

Tammy continued through her tears. "He told her if she ever told her mother, he would kill her and Tori. Molly was terrified. She was only eleven fucking years old. She told me after it happened a third time. She was sickened and disgusted with herself and blamed herself for everything. That was his doing. He made her think it was her fault. Molly was already a very pretty girl and Lancaster told her it was her fault she was so 'irresistible.'"

"Fuck!" Ryder remembered the day he'd said that to her and how she froze. He thought it was weird at the time, but didn't think anything more of it.

Tammy continued, "The fourth time he forced himself on her, Molly's mother walked in and caught him. She hit him over the head with something and told him to get the fuck out of their house, or she would call the police. She said to never contact them again. He did leave, surprisingly. Tori blamed herself for Molly being abused. It was her fault, in a lot of ways. If she hadn't lied in the first place, Lancaster would have always known Molly wasn't his. It doesn't excuse his behavior."

Tammy twisted her fingers together so tightly they began turning red. "One day, Molly noticed him outside the school as we were leaving. It was about a year and a half later. We were almost thirteen. I told her she needed to tell someone—her mom, the police, the school, someone. But she refused. We started walking different ways home from school; I was always with her. I found a guy that could get us pepper spray and got us each several canisters of it. We carried them everywhere we went.

"Then, one day, we were at my house. We had seen him at school that day. We were scared and got a ride home from a guy in school who had a car. We ran into my house and locked all the doors and windows. Later, we were watching the television and a "news bulletin" came on and a picture of Lancaster was on the screen. He had grabbed another girl at school. She looked a lot like Molly. He had raped her. That girl went straight to the police, and they found Lancaster a few hours later because of the announcement on the news.

"Molly always blamed herself for that girl being raped. If she'd turned him in when it happened to her, that girl wouldn't have been hurt. Tori felt the same way. She started drinking heavier and heavier. My mom insisted that Molly stay with us most of the time. She ate every meal with us and slept in my room with me. We were inseparable. I never wanted Molly out of my sight."

Ryder stood quickly and paced the floor a few times. He rotated his head and stretched his shoulders. His eyes sought his brothers', and their eyes showed sadness and anger for a pretty little girl whose innocence was taken far too early.

Tammy continued, "After Lancaster had gone to jail, she felt safer. She would stay at my house, check on her mom most days, only to find her drunk or with some guy. Tori started running through guys like crazy. Molly, of course, didn't want to be in the house with any of those men, especially after what had happened to her. She started using Bates as her last name because she couldn't stand using Elson and she didn't know who her biological father was. Bates was Tori's mother's maiden name.

"A few years ago, Tori had a stroke, and it pushed her into the past, where it was probably the only time in her life that she'd been happy. That's why Molly was always so worried she would be like her mom. She never wanted to be that person."

Tammy was crying by the time she finished. Through her tears, she said, "I've never told anyone anything." Danny put his arms around her and whispered soft, sweet words in her ears.

The room was largely quiet. Joci sniffled a few times, quietly wiping her eyes with a tissue. Gunnar stood ramrod straight; his jaw clenched so tight it could rival Fort Knox. JT stood against a wall with his arms crossed, his stance wide. Jeremiah sat next to Joci on the sofa, opening and closing his fists, his breathing ragged.

Tammy composed herself after a bit. She wiped her eyes and tear stained cheeks, then said, "She's a good person, Ryder. She would never do anything to hurt you. She's been hurt so much in her short life." She hiccupped from her crying. "Lancaster must have threatened her. That's the only reason she would have broken up with you. Please don't be mad at her; give her the chance to explain."

Ryder shook his head. This was un-friggin-real. His heart hurt for her. He had an idea she had suffered as a child. The revelation that she didn't have a Christmas tree when she was younger made him think as much. Part of him suspected she'd been abused, but he never went there. It would pop into his head, and he would push it right out. It was too horrific to think about. Right now, controlling the rage roiling through him seemed an impossible feat. How anyone, especially the man who had been a father for at least nine years, could turn on a little girl in such a vicious way, threatened to send him on a hunting rampage he'd never thought he was capable of.

He paced a few times, looked at his brothers and froze. They held his gaze for a long time, each silently communicating to him their support. He turned to Tammy, planted his hands on his hips and took a deep breath. "I love her, Tammy. All I've ever wanted was for her to let me in—share things with me."

# 21

## HOME

A couple of hours later, Molly walked into her kitchen to find a house full of people sitting there waiting for her. Tammy yelled, "They're here. She's home," as she sprung from the sofa and ran to the front door. She flung it open as an officer escorted Molly inside. As soon as he saw her, Ryder stood and stared. He was afraid to move toward her. He didn't know what he should do. His fists knotted at his side; his throat convulsed as he swallowed, unable to dislodge the knots there.

Molly froze at the sight of him. He wasn't moving toward her, just staring. Tears welled up in her eyes as she watched him swallow. He took a step forward and the dam burst. She ran into his arms, a blubbering pile of hot mess. He wrapped his arms around her and kissed the top of her head. She hung on tight, her body shaking from the emotions of the past few days.

"I'm so sorry, Ryder. He told me he would kill you if I didn't get rid of you. I couldn't let him hurt you. I'm so sorry."

Ryder shushed Molly and softly whispered in her hair, "It's all right, babe. Please don't cry. We'll figure it all out."

But the most important thing Ryder said to Molly was, "I love you, Molly—so damn much."

She raised her head and looked into his eyes—they looked tired, obviously showing his lack of sleep, mixing with his pain, sorrow and loss. After what she'd done, she couldn't blame him for being mad at her. But she would do anything she could to make it up to him. She wasn't letting this man go. Not now. Not ever.

"I love you, too. I'm so sorry." The damn burst again, and this time it was more from fatigue and relief than fear.

Ryder looked at the bruise forming on the side of her face. With gentle fingers, he touched the purplish skin on her cheek and with a whisper-soft graze, he kissed the spot where his fingers just were. He leaned down and kissed her. His lips shook, but he felt compelled to touch his lips to hers.

Tammy came pushing forward. "You can have her to yourself later. Right now, I need to hug my girl."

She grabbed Molly and hugged her so hard Molly had trouble breathing. Tammy pulled away after a bit and looked at her. "Are you okay, Moll? He didn't hurt you, did he?"

Molly shrugged, and Tammy's eyes zoned in on the bruise forming on her cheek. "Something snapped in me. I just couldn't let him touch me. He threatened to kill Ryder if I didn't do what he wanted, but I just couldn't let him touch me again. I decided I wasn't going to be his victim anymore. I wasn't going to hide while he hurt other people."

Tammy hugged Molly again and then pulled back. "I told them, Moll. Ryder wanted to know, and I felt I had to say something. I'm sorry I broke your confidence, but you should have told him a long time ago. Secrets hurt people."

"I know, Tammy. I'm sorry to make you go through that awful story. Don't worry; I know you wouldn't have said anything unless you felt it was necessary."

Before any more words could be said, Joci pushed her way forward and pulled Molly into a hug. Jeremiah followed as well as JT, and finally Gunnar.

"Glad to see you back, sis. I was worried about you. We all were." He held her shoulders in his palms and stared intently at her face.

She looked into his eyes, so much like her own, while a sad smile formed on her face. "I'm glad to be back. I'm sorry I worried anyone. It wasn't my intent."

"Let's sit and talk, shall we?" Joci pulled a chair out to sit down. "We need to discuss this. Then Molly and Ryder will need to have a private conversation, just the two of them."

They each found a spot at the table or around the room, quietly respectful.

Molly looked around at each of them, then up at Ryder and held those sad eyes with her own. "I owe you all an explanation, please ask any questions you want me to answer. I've just learned, for the second time in my life, how dangerous secrets can be." She looked at Gunnar and then Joci. "I want to get everything out in the open and not have anyone speculate on anything."

Tammy reached across the table and took Molly's hand. "How did he find you, Molly?"

Her lips thinned into a straight line. "He found me from my name and picture on the Rolling Thunder Veteran's Ride DVD. I don't know how he came to see that—who knows how many people have that DVD and sent it to people they know. It doesn't matter. The first time he called, he told me how he found me. He called my business number."

Tammy gasped. "I'm so sorry, Moll."

Molly shook her head before she got the words out.

"No. You do not say that. How could you know? Since he didn't go to prison for raping me, I wouldn't be on the police list for them to notify me of his release. And I should have been a little more mindful of the time he spent there and the fact that he would be getting close to his release date."

Joci asked, "What about your mom, Molly? Does she remember him?"

Molly gasped. "He went to see her. When he called me, I asked him not to go to her, but he did anyway. I don't know if she remembers him. He's the reason she started drinking in the first place. She felt so bad about his abuse of me; she just couldn't forgive herself. I need to go to the nursing home and make sure she's okay and speak with the staff to see what her reaction was to him."

Ryder gave her a gentle squeeze. His throat was thick with emotion and he couldn't say much. He was dumbfounded at the whole situation. He felt so much love toward her to think that she put herself in harm's way to protect him. But he was pissed, too. She shouldn't have put any of them through this. Then again, it's hard to rely on people when you've never had anyone to rely on. She had Tammy, but she was it all these years. His head was a mess right now.

They spoke for a couple of hours, but it didn't feel like it'd been that long. Molly had to admit, it felt so good to get everything off her chest. To be able to tell people who loved her what she had gone through was so freeing.

After everyone hugged Molly again and told her they loved her, she and Ryder were left alone to discuss what had happened. This was the hardest conversation of all because Molly didn't know if Ryder still wanted to be with her after this. She had treated him terribly. Of all of the people in the world that deserved to be hurt, this man was not one of them. She felt her own heart break at what she'd done to Ryder.

"Where should we sit to talk?"

Ryder motioned to the living room and took a deep breath. "Why don't we sit on the sofa? My ass is sore from sitting on those kitchen chairs all day."

She smiled and nodded, grabbed a bottle of water and motioned to Ryder. He held up a bottle he already had in his hand in answer. They sat on the sofa; each turned facing the other.

He swallowed hard. "Did you want to break up with me?"

She pleaded with her eyes for him to believe her. "No. I didn't want Lancaster to hurt you. I didn't know what to do; he's a terrible man and I know firsthand that he doesn't have regard for his actions."

He shook his head; his lips formed a straight line. "Why did you leave a note, Molly? Why didn't you talk to me in person?"

She scrunched up her face, tears threatening behind her eyes. "I knew I couldn't say it in person and be convincing. There was nothing in the world I hated doing more than leaving that note, but in the end, I was so afraid. I thought once you knew about my past, you wouldn't want me anyway, so I thought it was probably already over."

"Molly..." Ryder swallowed. "I would never not want you. You were a kid, for crying out loud. Why would you think I would ever hold anything against you that happened to you when you were a kid?" His voice trembled, and his jaw tightened.

She didn't think she had any tears left; she had cried them all out today. But hearing his sweet words just now made her feel like crying. She stared into his eyes, a thousand thoughts running through her mind at once. She loved this man before her, never dreamed she could love someone so much.

He leaned forward and cupped her face in his hands. "I love you, Molly Bates, with my whole heart and my whole soul. The shitty things that happened to you as a child are over. But right now, I need time away from you."

She choked back a sob and swiped at an errant tear trailing its way across her bruised cheek. "I...understand."

"You didn't talk to me. You should have told me a long time ago. If you can't trust me with your deep dark secrets, how can we move forward?"

She pleaded for him to believe her. "Ryder. I'm so damn sorry. Of all the people in the world who don't deserve to be hurt, you are that person. I..." Swallowing hard, she looked down at her hands as they twisted together, knuckles white with strain. "I'm sorry," she whispered.

"I know you are, but you broke my fucking heart, Molly." He stood to leave, walked toward the kitchen, then paused and looked back at her. "I just need some time to think."

She looked up as he rounded the corner. She heard the door to the garage shut. Several minutes went by before she heard his truck start. She stood and walked to the window and watched as Ryder pulled out of the driveway, and without looking back at the house, he drove away from her.

## 22

## HOW DO YOU MEND A BROKEN HEART?

Ryder lie in his old bed at Gunnar and JT's and stared at the ceiling. He didn't know how long he'd been lying there. He felt numb. He hadn't eaten in two—no, three days. It didn't matter; time just crawled by. As he lie there thinking about Molly, he jumped up and walked over to his dresser. Sliding the top drawer open, he pulled out his notebook. Turning and crossing the room, he flopped down into a chair and threw his legs up on the bed. Taking a deep breath, he opened his notebook and started writing.

∾

Molly paced back and forth in Tammy and Danny's living room. "I wish you would stop that pacing. You're driving me crazy."

Molly stopped and looked at Tammy. With a heavy sigh, she walked to the love seat in front of the big picture window and flopped down. "Sorry. He won't return any of my calls. It's been four days. I've left hundreds of messages. Well, dozens, anyway."

"He said he needed to think. You hurt him bad, Molly. He's sensitive and shy. This was a real blow to him. You should have seen him; he was wrecked."

Molly let her head fall back against the back of the sofa and looked out the window. The beautiful flowers were all gone for the winter now. Brown, shriveled and dried up. Just like she felt. Lifeless. She felt her phone vibrate in her pocket and pulled it out. When she saw Gunnar's picture on her phone, she pursed her lips, touched the "answer" icon and lifted the phone to her ear. "Hi, Gunnar."

"Hang on there, I have to get over the excitement in your voice before I can continue," he snarked.

"Sorry. I always want to talk to you. I was just hoping Ryder would finally be ready to talk to me."

"That's why I'm calling. He hasn't left his room since he came back here. He hasn't eaten anything. JT and I are worried sick about him, and my mom is going crazy trying to get him to open up. He called in sick to work today again. Something has to be done. I have an idea."

"Okay, what can I do?"

"Come over to the house. JT and I will leave when you get here and give you two time to talk. You'll have to force the issue. Make him talk to you."

"I can do that." Molly sat up straight, feeling hopeful for the first time in days. "I'll be there in a few minutes."

~

Ryder turned his head to look at the back of the bedroom door. Someone was knocking again. "What?" Taking a deep breath, he said, "Leave me alone. Fuck! Please, just leave me alone."

"No can do, brother." Gunnar stuck his head in the door. "JT and I are heading out to The Barn. We'll see you later, okay?"

"Yeah. Later."

Gunnar stepped back and motioned for Molly to enter Ryder's room. When Ryder saw her walk in, he sat up and looked at Gunnar, narrowing his eyes at his brother. Gunnar smirked and walked out the door.

Molly stepped in farther and closed the door behind her. "I couldn't wait any longer to see you. Please talk to me."

"If you don't trust me enough to tell me *everything*, we can't possibly have a solid relationship when only *one* of us is giving everything."

Molly gingerly sat at the foot of the bed and twisted her body, so she was facing him. "I've learned my lesson. I'm here to swear to you there will never be secrets between us again. Except maybe Christmas and birthday presents." Flashing her brightest smile, she focused all of her attention on his eyes.

He scraped his hands down his face and around to the back of his neck. He rotated his head to relieve the stiffness that had formed over the past few days.

She leaned forward and laid her palm on Ryder's shin. Squeezing gently, she took a deep breath. "I know I hurt you. If I could take it back, I would in a heartbeat. I'm not used to having so many people care about me. All I've ever had was Tammy, and she's with Danny now, so... I thought I was protecting you, Ryder. I honestly did."

He stared at her. She saw him swallow the lump in his throat. The clock ticked in the corner of the room, the tree outside the window swayed gracefully as a breeze swept by. "Molly." Taking another breath, he tried again. "I still love you, but I can't go through anything like that ever again. It's the worst feeling in the world, thinking you're not good enough for the person you love. I thought I wasn't good enough for you to tell me the truth."

She shook her head as he spoke. "I know all too well what it feels like to think you're not good enough for the person you love. Look at you and your family. They're amazing. Even though you've all dealt with shit, it's nothing like my life. I didn't come to you a virgin. I felt dirty and unworthy. I was afraid every damn day that you would find out about me and dump me because I was filthy." She swallowed. "I know what that's like more than you ever will."

Wiping at the tears that streamed down her face, she stood to leave. She paused with her hand on the doorknob and turned. "You know, you don't tell me everything either," she said, pointing to the top of his dresser, where his notebook sat. "You write your deepest, darkest thoughts in the journal over there, and you never share them. You're no different than me when it comes to keeping secrets. Granted, my secrets caused other people to get hurt. This time, I hoped it would be different and no one would suffer. I was wrong."

She turned the knob on the door, and walked out of the room, then left the house. She climbed into her car, surprised that the tears had stopped. She'd tried everything she could; this was her last stand. He simply didn't want her anymore. She drove home to her little house with a heavy heart.

She walked into her small house feeling lost. She hadn't been back here since the night Ryder left. The house felt creepy to her now. She began emptying the dishwasher when the kitchen door flew open behind her. She jumped and spun around and froze as her eyes met Ryder's. Gently laying the plate in her hand on the counter so she wouldn't drop it, she smoothed her blouse with her hands and waited for what he came to say.

"Are you always going to run away from me when things get tough?"

"No...I didn't." Molly stammered.

"You didn't? Yes. You. Did. I wasn't finished talking to you. You turned, accused me of betraying you and walked out." Ryder's nostrils flared. Molly had never seen him angry. It was...scary.

"I'm...I'm..." Taking a deep breath, Molly tried again. "I'm sorry. I didn't think you wanted to talk to me anymore."

Ryder closed his eyes and ran his hand down his face trying to compose himself. He was scaring her. Running his hand over his throat and around to his nape, he let out a breath. He opened his eyes and watched Molly's throat convulse with fear. "Fuck!" He said as he stepped closer to her.

She stepped back as he stepped forward. He halted for a millisecond, then stepped forward again—two steps, three steps, until they were toe to toe.

"What I wanted to say was, we should start over. You're right. I wasn't completely open with you, either."

A sob tore out of Molly's throat as she flung herself into his arms. He held her close; one arm wrapped around her waist, his other palm pressing her head into his chest. Long seconds passed before he could loosen his hold on her.

"I love you, Molly. I have from the first day I saw you."

She tilted her head back to look into his sexy face, ravaged by lack of sleep and food, and filled with worry. Her fingers gently brushed along his jaw and over his lips. Reaching up, she placed a feather light kiss on his lips as her hands held his head in hers.

"I love you, too, Ryder." Molly's voice was barely a whisper; her throat was so constricted.

He kissed her. Slowly and sweetly, he touched his lips to hers and softly made love to her mouth. He dipped his tongue into her mouth and swirled it around. He'd missed this woman. He slid his hands to her waist and pulled her into his body. He walked them into the living room and leaned back on the sofa, pulling her down on top of him. She froze, looked back at the windows and then at Ryder.

"Lancaster told me he watched us make love under the tree. Are there cameras in here? What about the microphone from Jepson? This place feels kind of creepy now, doesn't it?"

"Haven't you been staying here?"

"No. I went to Tammy's as soon as you left. She told me about Jepson."

Ryder snorted a little. "Yeah, I have to say, it does feel creepy. Why don't we go to a hotel? Just me and you and spend a couple of days making up for lost time?"

Molly grinned. "Actually, that sounds great. I know we have to get back here and deal with all of this..." she swept her hand out wide "... stuff. Cameras, fear, everything—but a few days alone together, getting ourselves right sounds better to start with."

"Okay, let's scoot. I really need to make up for lost time."

## 23

## NEW BEGINNINGS

Molly stood in the shower and let the hot water pour over her. What a crazy ass few days they had. She started the day, her second without a shower, feeling dark and depressed and scared. She was going to end the day in the arms of the man she loved more than her own life. But first, she had to get cleaned up. It felt like a little slice of heaven standing here with the water flowing over her body. This morning felt like it was weeks ago with all that had happened. She lathered her hair up and rinsed it out. She soaped and shaved and rinsed again.

As she stepped out of the shower, she genuinely felt like herself again. She quickly applied body butter and blew her hair dry. Taking a deep breath, she opened the door and stepped out expecting to see Ryder. He wasn't there. She looked to the right, where the bed sat behind a half wall. Gawd, there he was, this perfect man. He was propped against the pillows, naked and waiting for her. She looked at him, admiring the beauty of his body and watched as his cock came to life in front of her. She watched in fascination as it grew harder and harder. Without even thinking, she licked her lips, imagining his cock sliding into her mouth, making it twitch and grow harder still.

She looked into Ryder's eyes and saw him watching her. He looked at her breasts, then lower, staring at her pussy. Slowly, his eyes traveled back up her body and stilled on her eyes.

Would he ever get enough of looking at this woman? Her small face with those sky blue eyes and her full lips, always ready to smile. He loved how her dark hair and lashes framed those blue eyes. Her pussy? Well, it was to die for. Nothing felt better than sliding into her pussy. She clenched him tightly with a velvet smoothness that brushed along the skin of his cock like nothing ever could. Usually, by the time he pushed into her, his cock was throbbing and hard and aching for release. When he slid into her slickness, he had to blank his mind for fear of losing control and coming on the spot.

He watched her like a starving man eager for his meal. She stopped alongside the bed and reached out and wrapped her hand around his cock. It jerked at her touch, but she smiled and began sliding her hand up and down its length. He looked into her eyes and saw happiness once again. He reached out and slid his forefinger along the seam of her pussy, then gently pushed inside of her. She smirked at him and slowly leaned forward and slid her mouth over the head of his cock. He groaned loudly as the wet warmth of her greedy mouth pleasured him.

They'd been without each other for only a little more than a week, but still, this probably wouldn't last long. They usually made love at least once—if not more—each day. She cupped his balls with one hand and slid her other hand up and down his length with her mouth, keeping him completely covered. She pulled him out of her mouth and licked down the underside and then licked his balls. He put his hand on her head and held her there. A groan escaped his lips as he let his mind float to the pleasure she was offering him.

She continued licking his balls and running her hand up and down his length slowly, making love to him with her mouth. She ran her tongue around his cock again and pulled him into her mouth with gentle suction, making him raise his hips in the air, pushing up into her mouth. His hand became more insistent on her head, pushing her faster. She continued stimulating him with her moans while sucking and applying more pressure. With his assistance, her movements increased in speed. He could feel his balls scrunching up into his body, and she smiled at him. He began shaking, trying to control his reaction to her, but it was proving impossible.

He hadn't had her in a few days, and he knew this would be short lived. As she moaned and sucked on him, it was all he could do not to shoot into her mouth the first time. She continued to suck and moan and dammit, he was so horny it was almost too much. Molly moved a little, and her breasts rubbed against his leg, and that was all it took. He spurt into her mouth with a loud groan.

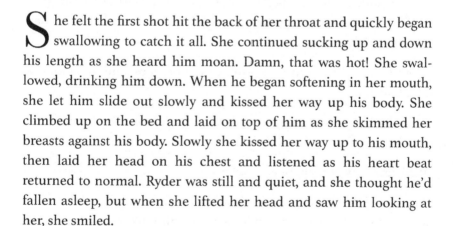

She felt the first shot hit the back of her throat and quickly began swallowing to catch it all. She continued sucking up and down his length as she heard him moan. Damn, that was hot! She swallowed, drinking him down. When he began softening in her mouth, she let him slide out slowly and kissed her way up his body. She climbed up on the bed and laid on top of him as she skimmed her breasts against his body. Slowly she kissed her way up to his mouth, then laid her head on his chest and listened as his heart beat returned to normal. Ryder was still and quiet, and she thought he'd fallen asleep, but when she lifted her head and saw him looking at her, she smiled.

"I thought you fell asleep."

"No. I was just enjoying you on top of me. I missed you, Molly. So damn much. I thought my heart would never heal, and the hurt would always be there. You crushed me. And just now, you crushed me again. Only this time, it was sweet and loving and tender. It felt so fucking good that my mind took longer to catch up to what my body was feeling."

"I'm so sorry, babe. I never wanted to hurt you. I really thought I was doing what was necessary to keep you safe."

He cupped her face in his hands. "I know, Molly. I do. But, never, ever do that to me again. Do you hear me? I won't survive next time."

A single tear slid down her cheek. Ryder quickly swiped it away with his thumb. "No more tears. Let's promise to never again keep secrets from each other. If there is anything bothering either of us, we talk about it; we don't run. If there is an issue, we fix it, we don't run. Mostly, we never run."

She nodded and grinned. "I promise. I will never run again. I swear on my life."

He quickly flipped her over, so he was on top of her. He held her with his arms under her. He wiggled around, so her legs were spread apart and he was lying between them. He was still chest to chest with her, looking deeply into her eyes.

"I love looking into your eyes, Molly. I want to look into them for the rest of my life."

"I love looking into your eyes, Ryder. I want to look into them for the rest of my life."

"Well, let's make that happen, shall we?"

She giggled. He kissed his way down her beautiful body. He suckled her breasts and rolled her nipples between his fingers and thumb. He kissed his way down her stomach, across her hips and to the apex of her thighs. He was treated to the most beautiful view of looking up at Molly and seeing her large breasts, with nipples puckered tight. She watched him with those big blue eyes, and never breaking his gaze, he licked her pussy and watched her pupils dilate and her nostrils flare. He grinned and licked her again.

"Do you realize what a view I have here? Fucking beautiful. You are the most beautiful woman I've ever laid eyes on, Molly."

He slid down an inch or so and began licking her in earnest. He parted her folds, watching intently as he did. What a beautiful sight this was. He watched as his fingers slid across her moist flesh and listened to her moans as he did. He saw the glistening flesh and reached out with his tongue to taste her honey. He slowly slid two fingers into her wetness and reveled in her moans. He watched his fingers sliding in and out of her, giving her pleasure. It was beautiful. He could feel the walls of her pussy constrict as he slid his fingers out and it made his cock twitch. He slid his fingers back in and listened to Molly moan again. As he pushed his fingers inside and curled them just a little to hit her g-spot deep inside, she quivered and groaned. That was the spot. Her breathing staggered and came in fast huffs. He looked up her body and saw that she was beginning to glow with a fine sheen of sweat. He slid his fingers out and back in, curling them just a bit and elicited yet more groans of satisfaction. Yes, perfect. A few more times and she came apart in his hands, and he'd barely put his tongue on her clit. He slid his fingers out of her and replaced them with his tongue, so he could taste her sweet honey.

He slid up her body and kissed her softly as he pushed himself inside of her. They both groaned as he entered her. Good God, this was the best feeling in the world.

## 24

## RYDER'S NOTEBOOK:

"Here's a good one. It's in Mom and Dad's neighborhood and not far from JT and Gunnar."

Ryder sat at the kitchen table with his laptop. He and Molly had decided they no longer wanted to stay in this house. It didn't matter that they could get a great deal on it; it just seemed tainted now.

Molly wiped her hands on a towel, walked up behind him and wrapped her arms around his shoulders. "That does look good. Let's scroll through the pictures."

They clicked through the images. "Wow, that looks great, I think we should go see it." He reached for his phone and began dialing a number.

Molly went back to preparing breakfast. She listened to Ryder make an appointment with a realtor to look at the house. She put the bacon in the microwave and took two plates from the cupboard and set them on the counter.

She glanced at the Christmas tree in the living room. They had decorated it and installed a security system so they would know if anyone was in the house. They changed the blinds in the living room and kitchen so no one could see in the house. They didn't have to give any notice. Jepson wasn't in jail, but there was a restraining order on him, and they didn't owe that bastard anything.

Ryder ended his call and said, "Two hours and we can go see it." He stood and closed the lid on his laptop. "Before we go looking at houses, I want to show you something. I'll be right back." He walked to the bedroom. Molly watched him disappear through the doorway and smiled. She set the plates on the table and turned when he returned and laid a notebook on the table.

She looked at the notebook and then back up to Ryder.

She grinned. "You want to show me your notebook?"

He nodded. "When I first met you, I was shy and couldn't bring myself to ask you out. My mom told me to write things down that maybe I would feel like we had already had a conversation and it wouldn't be so scary talking to you. I did, I started writing things down. I want you to read them. My thoughts. No secrets, remember?"

He pushed the notebook forward and winked at her. She pulled a chair from the table and slid the notebook toward her and paused, unsure if she should read Ryder's thoughts. She looked back up at him, and he nodded and smiled.

She opened the cover of the notebook and began reading.

*September 28 – I met a woman today. The most beautiful woman I've ever seen. Besides my mom of course. Her name is Molly Bates. She has the bluest eyes I've ever seen. Dark brown hair, so shiny it gleams. She has full kissable lips, and when she smiles, she takes my breath away. Of course, I couldn't ask her out. Why would she go out with me anyway? She's hot. I know I'm not bad, but someone like her, well, she probably has men begging her to go out with them.*

Molly looked up at Ryder, and he nodded to the notebook, wanting her to continue.

*October 5 a.m. – I haven't had the courage to ask Molly out. I want to so bad. I've thought of her all week. Every day I wake up thinking about her. Every night I go to sleep thinking about her. I want to know all about her. What does she like? What does she think? Is she interested in me?*

*October 5 p.m. – I brought her home with me tonight. She was drunk and some asshole tried molesting her. I knocked him on his ass and brought her home so no one else would hurt her. I've been sitting in this chair for hours watching her sleep. She's so beautiful. She looks peaceful sleeping. Her face is soft and relaxed, and it makes my cock hard and my stomach flip-flop to look at her lying in my bed. She's in MY bed. The only thing that could make this better would be me lying next to her with my arms around her. I've never felt like this about anyone before. It scares me a little, but it also excites me to think about being in love. Not sure if that's what it is, but it sure is nice.*

*October 6 – Molly came on a bike ride with my family and me today. It was bittersweet having her on my bike. She felt so good behind me with her arms wrapped around me. I could feel her breasts pushing into my back and her legs wrapped around me, and it felt...right. It was also hard but, well, I was hard. All fucking day I had a cock so hard I could hammer nails with it. Every time I heard her laugh, every time she climbed on my bike and wrapped her arms around me. Every time she said something in my ear, my cock twitched and throbbed. Bittersweet is a great way to describe today.*

*October 13 – Yesterday I made love for the first time in my life. I know I made love to Molly, because I've never, ever felt like that with anyone before. I never will again. Dad was right; you know it when it hits you. That's what he told me when I asked him how he knew Joci was the one for him. He said, "I just knew. You will too, you'll know it when it hits you." I got hit today with the love bug or whatever. It doesn't feel scary like I thought it would. It feels good actually. The only thing that feels bad is the uncertainty. I have no idea how Molly feels. It's too soon to have that conversation. But I do know I can't wait to see her later today. We have to work at the build again today. Tonight, Mom and Dad want us all to come over for dinner and enjoy each other since we've been working so hard. Mom seems to like Sunday dinners. It seems like it might be the start of a nice family tradition. I'm asking Molly to join us for family dinner. She fits with all of us and I really want to spend the time with her.*

*November 7 – Molly and I have spent almost every day together since the first time we made love. I never knew life could be like this. So amazing. I look forward to waking up every morning so I can see her and spend time with her. She's funny. She has a great personality. She's smart, beautiful, actually, she's perfect. I'm in love, madly in love with Molly Bates.*

*November 12 – I told Molly that I loved her today, and she told me she loved me as well. We're moving in together, and I can't wait. I'm going to marry that girl as soon as I can. Is there a time frame you have to wait to ask the woman you love to marry you? My dad asked Joci within a few months, maybe three or four, of them actually dating. He didn't want to wait anymore for her to be his wife. I don't want to wait either, but I'm not sure how Molly feels about that.*

*November 13 – Molly's landlord died, and his son came to the house today to discuss Molly purchasing the house. He's a creepy fuck, and he had Molly cornered in the kitchen when I walked in. I'm so damn glad I got there in time. I hate to think what would have happened if I didn't come home. I would have to kill that son of a bitch if he had touched her. She's mine. She's the love of my life, and I'll hurt anyone that hurts her.*

*November 15 – Molly and Gunnar are brother and sister. No shit. We were celebrating Gunnar's adoption at Mom and Dad's house. Gunnar had a box from his biological dad's wife with pictures in it. He asked Mom to look at it with him and Molly saw a picture of her mom. One thing led to another, and now Mom thinks Keith is also Molly's dad. Friggin unreal. We're going to see Molly's mom and find out. She's nervous. I'm excited for her and Gunnar. They'll each have each other as well as all of us. Now that I look at both of them, I see it. It seems weird that we never thought they looked like each other before. But, now, it's almost impossible not to see it.*

*November 17* – *I met Molly's mom today. She didn't even realize Molly and I were in the room, she was focused on Gunnar. Gunnar looks a lot like Keith and Tori zoned in on that immediately. I'm so proud of Molly, though. She sat there while her mom gushed over Gunnar and never shed a tear. I can't imagine sitting next to my mom, either of them, and have them not know who I am. My Molly is a strong woman. I love her more every day, as impossible as that seems.*

*November 19* – *We're celebrating my grandparents' fiftieth wedding anniversary tonight. Mom has been spending a lot of time helping my aunts plan this party. Molly's nervous, but I can't wait to introduce her to my whole family as my girlfriend. She's the most beautiful woman in the world and every day, I fall in love more and more. We still haven't told everyone I'm moving in and buying the house with her. We will after all of this stuff blows over with Gunnar and Molly and them being brother and sister. That will probably be the talk of the evening, and I know she's nervous about that. We have time. I'm trying to be patient, but sometimes it's hard. I want to shout it from the rooftops, "I'm in love with Molly Bates, and she loves me." Maybe I'll do that one day.*

*November 24* - *Jepson came to the house again today and scared the shit out of Molly. That bastard better not ever lay a hand on her. She's so special to me, and I don't want anything to happen to her. Ever. I'm going to talk to my Uncle Tommy to see what we can do.*

*December 4* – *We got our first Christmas tree today. It was fun to go out to the tree farm and cut down our first tree. Danny and Tammy got their first tree together today as well. Molly told me that since she was eleven, she hasn't had a tree. Something terrible happened to this woman, and I need to find out what it is so I can help her move past it. But, from this point forward, we are going to have big Christmas trees every year. We made love under the tree after Tammy and Danny left. It was amazing, hearing Molly moan as I made love to her, smelling the pine of the tree and feeling her body love me back. I don't have the words to explain how it feels when I'm with her, in her.*

*December 5 a.m.* – *Today is the deadline for Jeffrey Jepson to agree to the purchase price of the house. We haven't seen him since the day he was here and scared the crap out of Molly. He better not ever show up again. I didn't like the way he was looking at her, and he gave Molly the creeps, big time. Of course, who could blame him for being attracted to her? Have I said I love her? If not, I'm crazy in love with Molly Bates.*

*December 5 p.m.* – *My heart was broken today. I've heard people talk about a broken heart before and thought it was a bunch of crap. But now I know. My heart is broken into so many pieces; I don't know if it can ever be put back together. Molly left me a note today, telling me she was breaking up with me. I need to find her to make her tell me what happened. Everything was perfect yesterday, and I was planning in my mind how to ask her to marry me. Today, my world is black and gray.*

*December 8 a.m.* – *I've spent the past few days in the most agonizing turmoil any person could ever imagine. My heart is broken. I'm afraid I will never see my heart again. I'm afraid something horrible has happened to Molly. I'm scared that being afraid is how the rest of my life will be. I don't want to be scared; I want Molly back. I'll do anything to fix what I did wrong. I don't even know what that is, but I'll fix it. I can't eat, I can't sleep, I can't think. I feel stuck in a vortex that keeps spinning, never moving forward, never moving back, just spinning.*

*December 8 p.m.* – *I got Molly back today. She came home and told us all what had happened. She hasn't had a very easy life. But I walked away. She hurt me and now that I know she's safe, I want some time to try and puzzle out why she wouldn't be honest with me. She didn't trust me enough to tell me about her stepfather and the abuse he put her through. She didn't trust me to love her completely. She didn't trust me.*

*December 10* – *I can't eat. I can't sleep. I don't want to talk to anyone or see anyone. Molly has left dozens of messages on my phone, but dammit, my feelings are hurt. My heart hurts. I don't know how to make it stop hurting.*

*December 12 – Molly came to see me today. I was mean to her, and she left. Then I realized I was being stupid and petty and small. She came to see me, and I shunned her. Shame on me. Our future is in my hands now.*

*December 12 p.m. - My heart miraculously mended in the very first moment I hugged Molly to me. Her touch healed me and made my black and gray days turn into the most vivid color. I love Molly so much, I want to shout it to the world. We came to the hotel because the house felt creepy. We're going to spend a couple of days here, making up.*

*December 21 – Molly and I have decided to move and buy a different house. This one just has too much bad mojo. I love the thought of finding a house with her and making it ours together. I hope we find something very soon. Mostly, I want Molly to be my wife. Molly, when you read this, I want you to know that you are the best thing that has ever happened to me in my life. You met a shy man, frustrated with himself and you now live with a man who feels bold, strong, confident, but mostly in love. Your love, Molly, has made me the man I am today, the man I always wanted to be. I want to spend the rest of my life with you. Sharing each day with you, loving you, making love to you and hopefully, raising a family with you. Molly, will you marry me?*

The tears rained down her cheeks by the time she finished reading Ryder's thoughts. She had no idea he'd felt this way. It was humbling knowing how deeply he loved her. It was horrible knowing how much she'd hurt him. She loved him beyond words as well. She turned to see Ryder kneeling on one knee beside her. He smiled his beautiful, bright smile and grabbed her hands in his.

"Will you marry me, Molly?"

She sobbed and threw her arms around him. "Yes," she managed between sobs. Ryder slid his arms around her waist and pulled her close. They hung on to each other for a while, Molly trying to get herself under control. Finally, she felt she could speak. She sat back and wiped her eyes.

"I love you, Ryder. I love you so much."

He smiled and took her left hand in his. "I know you do. I love you, too."

He slipped a beautiful ring on her finger. She gasped when she looked at the sparkle. A beautiful, radiant cut diamond, more than a karat, a double band with pave-set diamonds along each band and a halo around the radiant cut diamond. It was without a doubt the most beautiful ring she'd ever seen.

"It's official now. You're going to be my wife."

She looked into his eyes and saw love and kindness. He wanted to marry her and have a family? She looked down at the ring and back up, and all she could say was, "Wow."

He kissed her lips, her nose, and her forehead. "I was going to wait until Christmas, but I didn't want to wait anymore. I know we haven't been together very long, so we don't have to get married right away. We can wait until summer or next year if you want. Just please don't make me wait forever."

She cupped his jaw in her hand and gazed into the green pools she loved so much. "Ryder. I'm speechless. Your notebook...it's beautiful. I don't have words to express my thoughts. I had no idea you had feelings like that. I don't feel deserving of you, of them." She swallowed the sob threatening to escape. "You're amazing to me. You make me feel...so much, but mostly, you make me feel loved. I want to make you feel loved, Ryder. I promise you, I will love you for the rest of my life."

"That's all I ask for, Molly."

He leaned in and kissed her, softly, gently. He looked into her eyes and smiled. "Sealed with a kiss."

He reached over and pulled a beautiful green box with a gold ribbon from one of the chairs at the table. He smiled as he handed it to her.

"For special occasions. The only occasion that will be more special than this is the day you marry me. I'll buy the whole store for you that day."

She sobbed and wiped her eyes. She kissed his beautiful lips, cheeks, chin, and each eyelid as she gently took the box from his hands. She carefully lifted the lid of the beautiful Seroogies box, and as the aroma of sweet dark chocolate wafted out, her stomach growled. He laughed as she lifted the first beautiful truffle from the box, unwrapped it, and held it to his lips.

"This is the most special, special occasion I have ever had in my life. I'm so happy I'm sharing it with you, Ryder Sheppard."

He bit into the smooth chocolate confection and watched as Molly ate the other half. He licked her lips and hummed his approval.

"Let's go look at some houses and stop by my parents' house and tell them we're getting married. When we come home, I'm going to eat the rest of those off your body."

Keep reading for a sneak peek at Danny and Tammy from Moving to Forever.

**DANNY TRIED TO BREATHE** through the pain of his heart slamming into his chest. Trying to clear the fog in his head, he listened to the sounds around him, trying to remember where he was. His skin wore a fine sheen of sweat as he swallowed rapidly to moisten his throat. His leg hurt and the ringing in his ears made him nauseous.

Nothing but the damn ringing in his ears. *Breathe, just breathe.* A sharp slap on the face had his eyes flying open, looking into Lex's face. Lex was yelling at him, but Danny couldn't hear a word. His mouth was moving, the chords were standing out in his neck, his eyes were wild...something was wrong. Terribly wrong. Danny's eyes darted behind Lex to see Coop and Dirks looking down at him. They wore blood and dirt and they looked scared shitless.

Danny closed his eyes. *Think, dammit, think. What the fuck happened?*

As his heartbeat began to slow and the ringing subsided, a whirring sound caught his attention. His eyelids were heavy as though something weighed them down and he struggled to open them. Then he remembered, he was deaf and Lex couldn't talk. Fuck! Did someone drug him? Danny's heart rate picked up as he fought against the fog in his brain. Trying to sit up, he felt strong hands push at his shoulders.

"Easy, Sergeant, take it easy, we've got you now. It'll be fine."

Danny looked up into dark brown eyes peering through a full face helmet. The man looked to be about his age, maybe a little older.

"It's going to be okay, Sergeant, we're flying you to base in Kandahar and from there, you'll be flown to Germany. Try and relax, we'll be there in a few minutes."

Danny looked to the man's left and saw a pole holding several bags of liquids and tubes running down to his arm. Behind the pole, he saw the sky and felt the pitch and sway of the helicopter. He tried sitting up again, but the man gently held him in place. "You'll need to lie down, Sergeant, we're almost there."

Finding his voice, Danny said. "My leg hurts. What happened? Where are my men?" He licked his lips and looked into those brown eyes, close to the color of his own. Pleading silently for information.

"Your unit hit an IED. One casualty, two injuries. You were hit in the leg, the rest of your men are back at camp. The other injury is flying right behind us."

IED, that's right. Pot or water was the usual question before going out on a mission. Pot was a primary crop in Afghanistan and the insurgents usually didn't blow up their own crops. So they were most often safe if they walked through the pot. Water meant slopping through trenches where IEDs were seldom placed. But today, they had to walk into a camp and check out the residents living there. Fuckers lured them in by pretending to be in need of assistance. He remembered watching Reed and Janus walk up ahead. They'd been laughing at a joke one of them had told when the explosion blasted the camp.

Danny flew through the air and landed in a heap, the wind knocked out of him, his heart racing, ears ringing. Fuck.

"Am I gonna lose it?" He waited with his breath held while the medic's eyes turned pitiful.

"Sorry, Sergeant, you already did."

Get book #3 Moving to Forever now.

# ALSO BY PJ FIALA

To see a list of all of my books with the blurbs go to: https://www.pjfiala.com/bibliography-pj-fiala/

You can find all of my books at https://pjfiala.com/books

**Romantic Suspense**

**Rolling Thunder Series**

Moving to Love, Book 1

Moving to Hope, Book 2

Moving to Forever, Book 3

Moving to Desire, Book 4

Moving to You, Book 5

Moving Home, Book 6

Moving On, Book 7

Rolling Thunder Boxset, Books 1-3

**Military Romantic Suspense**

**Second Chances Series**

Designing Samantha's Love, Book 1

Securing Kiera's Love, Book 2

Second Chances Boxset - Duet

**Bluegrass Security Series**

Heart Thief, Book One

Finish Line, Book Two

Lethal Love, Book Three

Wrenched Fate, Book Four

Bluegrass Security Boxset, Books 1-3

**Big 3 Security**

Ford: Finding His Fire Book One

Lincoln: Finding His Mark Book Two

Dodge: Finding His Jewel Book Three

Rory: Finding His Match Book Four

Big 3 Security Boxset, Books 1-3

**GHOST**

Defending Keirnan, GHOST Book One

Defending Sophie, GHOST Book Two

Defending Roxanne, GHOST Book Three

Defending Yvette, GHOST Book Four

Defending Bridget, GHOST Book Five

Defending Isabella, GHOST Book Six

**RAPTOR**

RAPTOR Rising - Prequel

Saving Shelby, RAPTOR Book One

# ENJOY THIS BOOK? YOU CAN MAKE A BIG DIFFERENCE

Reviews are the most powerful tools in my arsenal when it comes to getting attention for my books. As much as I'd like to, I don't have the financial muscle of a New York publisher. I can't take out full page ads in the newspaper or put posters on the subway.

(Not yet, anyway.)

But I do have something much more powerful and effective than that, and it's something that those big publishers would die to get their hands on.

**A committed and loyal bunch of readers.**

Honest reviews of my books help bring them to the attention of other readers.

If you've enjoyed this book I would be so grateful to you if you could spend just five minutes leaving a review (it can be as short as you like) on the book's vendor page. You can jump right to the page of your choice by clicking below.

Thank you so very much.

# MEET PJ

Writing has been a desire my whole life. Once I found the courage to write, life changed for me in the most profound way. Bringing stories to readers that I'd enjoy reading and creating characters that are flawed, but lovable is such a joy.

When not writing, I'm with my family doing something fun. My husband, Gene, and I are bikers and enjoy riding to new locations, meeting new people and generally enjoying this fabulous country we live in.

I come from a family of veterans. My grandfather, father, brother, two sons, and one daughter-in-law are all veterans. Needless to say, I am proud to be an American and proud of the service my amazing family has given.

My online home is https://www.pjfiala.com.
You can connect with me on Facebook at https://www.facebook.com/PJFialaı,
and
Instagram at https://www.Instagram.com/PJFiala.
If you prefer to email, go ahead, I'll respond - pjfiala@pjfiala.com.

Made in the USA
Monee, IL
30 August 2022

12847839R00128